STORM AND SANCTUARY
A DEATHLESS LOVE NOVELLA

ZORA FOX

WELCOME TO THE EIGHT REALMS

A land of gods and goddesses—a savage, beautiful collection of islands in the Corae Sea. The stories here are violent, with explicit sexual content not intended for anyone under 18. These books about deathless love feature dark, often twisted romances. Enter at your own risk.

ZENIA

Ruled by Thenios, God-King of lightning

APHRISO

Ruled by Cytherea, goddess of pleasure

ERISET

Contested land, ruled by Ares and Bellona, god and goddess of war

MENOS

Ruled by Scira, goddess of wisdom

NALIA

Ruled by Basileus, god of the ocean

HYPERION

Ruled by Lox, god of the sun

KANTHAROS

Ruled by Vesta, goddess of hearth and home

FAR REALM

Ruled by Hades, god of the dead

Content warnings for this story of deathless love: attempted sexual assault, death, explicit sex, language, and mentions of physical abuse and war-related trauma

VILET

The aching muscles in my arms and legs hardly responded as I kicked and pinwheeled through dirty sea water. At least it was cleaner than I was. The cool, salty water felt good against my skin, and if I stayed under, no one would know I'd been aboard that cargo ship.

Sailing across the Corae Strait in the pitch-black belly of a ship would make anyone hungry. Add to that having to be still and silent the whole way. It made any movement—even swimming through littered water—a relief.

I pried open my eyes and glanced up. Sunlight filtered down, along with floating particles of algae, food, and trash. *Almost there.*

I swam a little farther, but I was running out of air. I couldn't move fast enough. The water made my movements sluggish, and that delay grated against urgency. I hadn't had the chance to do much swimming in Eriset, not with the long hours and most beaches being reserved for Ares' favorites. It was a miracle I'd gotten this far.

Steeling myself, I swished my protesting limbs a few more times. My escape was a miracle I wouldn't waste.

A shadow slowly covered my body. The dock. It had to be. I was close enough to the surface that I'd have bumped into a hull if the shadow were a ship.

Safe enough.

I emerged face first and sucked in a gulp of air. Dust fell from the planks above my head, coating my cheeks. Above the water, shouts and bangs of cargo, tapping footsteps, and loud haggling made a cacophony so loud I doubted anyone heard me. I could only poke my head above the sloshing surf as I treaded water.

Aphriso. I'd made it. Well, almost.

A complicated blend of hope and guilt, fear and resolve, churned in my empty stomach. I'd reached Aphriso, the island without any wars, the trading post of the Eight Realms. Now, I just needed to find a place to emerge unseen and then find some food.

My legs were getting tired, but I spent a moment longer under the dock, scrubbing at my hair, my underarms, and stained spots on my clothes. The air smelled like smoke and bird droppings, but I took a big breath of it before going under again.

It didn't take long to find a spot where a building would shield my exit from the water. *Being dripping wet just might give me away, though.* Mentally, I rolled my eyes at myself. But a little part of me burned like a candle. Colors were brighter. Even that smell tasted like possibilities. I was really, honestly close to finding somewhere Ares might not chase me. King Ares himself would never bother with someone like me, but a missing member of the armorer's guild? Even human, I was too valuable a resource not to be missed. One of his soldiers or underlings would look for me.

I'd had no choice when I was impressed for service at twelve. Neither had my brother Vash. He was pretty poetic, actually, compared to me, at least, and they had him apprentice with a ropemaker. All hands had to be ready to help with the war. As if it would ever end between the War Twins. They were gods of destruction and lived up to their name.

I tipped my head up toward the sun. It was a dry day for a port town. Once I squeezed out my dress and brown hair, they didn't look as wet as I feared they might. The structures here were small, outbuildings for all the trade going on here, probably. When I peeked around the corner, green mountains rose just ahead. Below them were steep rocky paths and finally the bustling port filled with crates and burly sailors.

My chest seized. Men like that could pass for soldiers. Enough of them came into the armory, and I never wanted to see another member of the Twin Armies as long as I lived. They were cruel and violent and looked at me with a special kind of greed.

I breathed slowly in and out, steadying myself. Sliding back behind the building, I scanned the ground, the wall, anywhere that could provide something helpful. Pounded into the wall but decaying now was a heavy metal ring. Poor blacksmithing had made it crack on top. I could probably yank it off if I pulled hard enough, but no one in Ares' territories used metal when they could help it. Ares' power could manipulate metal without even touching it. One time, a disgruntled soldier brought in an arm cuff that had melted into a lumpy ball. He made sure we all know how angry he was. Pretty sure the little scar by my ear was from him.

Biting my lip, I didn't see anything else that looked useful. Besides, my stomach was screaming for food. Everything else had to wait.

I'd be careful as I looked for a bite. Leaning out to see across the dock, which seemed like the only way to reach the paths up to the more secluded mountains, I found something. Chickens! Where there were chickens, there were usually eggs. Maybe it was an entire food shipment. Animals had to eat too, didn't they? And the chicken crates, stacked beside a guard-house wall, were high enough that I could hide behind those if I needed to.

I emerged, walking as quickly and casually as I could. The damp fabric of my dress slapped against my sore legs, but I was drying out more quickly than I expected.

Huge ships, like the one where I'd lay tucked next to cargo for two days, butted up to the dock. Loud voices shouted and laughed. Hairy hands gripped thick ropes and hauled boxes ashore.

Air wouldn't enter my lungs the right way. I kept seeing eyes following me as I moved. *Faster. It'll be fine. You're seeing things.*

By the time I ducked behind the tower of chicken crates, I regretted not bringing that metal ring. I was alone in a strange place. What was I thinking not bringing protection?

I'll find something. I'll make it. My mind flew to Vash. *And then I'll get you here somehow.* Vash would know what to do. Or, if he didn't, at least he'd be calm and collected, with that smile that always threatened to break out on his face but rarely showed all the way. Hurt that had nothing to do with hunger pierced my body.

I shouldn't have told him I was leaving. Now, soldiers could torture the information out of him. All at my expense. But he'd told me to run, go, be safe. He was excited for me.

My stomach roiled with hard-edged guilt. Vash was the only family I had left. Part of me wished I had stayed, for his sake, but the bigger part felt utterly relieved to have escaped. Was it right to feel relieved when I had only saved myself? What was I worth compared to everyone else back home praying the next day didn't bring horrific violence? Shouldn't I go back to them?

I blew out a breath. In a second, I'd move on. No food here, like I'd hoped. Even the eggs had been cleaned out. I rummaged beneath a few hens just to be sure.

I wasn't fully concealed here, but this was still better than being out in the open until I collected myself. If anyone found out about me, where I'd come from...

The hill rose steeply away from the dock. Beyond that were green mountains. Cytherea's realm. She was the goddess of love. That meant that somewhere on this island, I could hopefully find the peace I craved. At least Aphriso wasn't at war. There was a jagged difference between fearing that Ares' army could massacre me and all my neighbors, and navigating a sketchy port town.

I'd take the sketchy port town.

"No need to hide, lovely."

The sneering words came from a grinning man with glittering eyes, probably twice my age. His uneven sunburnt skin and mismatched clothing showed he was a sailor.

My breath stopped.

Did he know? Would he send me back to earn some kind of reward from Ares?

My heart hammered so hard I felt my pulse in my ears.

A second man joined the first. His curiosity turned to delight when he saw me. This one was taller, darker, with a scraggly beard. I recognized the greed in the men's eyes.

No, gods.

"Are you stuck back there? You're going to get chicken shit all over your dress."

Why had I penned myself in? At my back was a stone wall. In front of me were the crates. I had a sliver of room to my left, but that just fed back to the dock, not away up the hill.

"I'm fine," I said, my voice hoarse and breathy. "Just unloading."

Twin grins at that, as merciless as the Twin Armies back home.

I was so close to freedom, so close! I couldn't lose my chance now.

They took a step forward. Another. My heartbeat thrashed.

"I know a place that would take care of you, get you cleaned up and all that." It was as if I'd never given my excuse. But I was afraid to push the issue because my accent might give me away. Did people here speak the same way? It was hard to tell with the leer in these sailor's voices.

"You're pretty enough to make good money," the bearded one added. "That's lucky for you. It's harder to help the ugly ones."

Bile pressed against the center of my throat. My gaze

dashed to the left. Other sailors worked there, all sweaty muscle. Would they help or gang up on me? I had to assume the second one. No one even seemed to notice my predicament.

In my experience, strangers killed. Strangers stole. Strangers raped.

At home, war between the gods meant that humans, like me, were caught in the middle. Some survived by taking a side and earning a god's protection, and others survived by agreeing with whoever held the most power that day. Neither position guaranteed safety. The best chance at life was to get away.

So I would get away.

The two men stalked closer.

With a shriek, I shoved the chicken crates toward them. Birds squawked. Feathers flew. I ran as fast as I could around the guardhouse. As long as there wasn't a wall on the other side or something, I could race up the hill and—

Thick fingers gripped my forearm, yanking me backward. A hand closed over my mouth, smothering my scream. I flailed and thrashed, but the hands were strong. They smelled like old potato skins.

He wrestled me into the alley behind the guardhouse. There was a wall there after all. Not a very tall one, but enough to shelter this spot from view. Building on one side, walls on two others. The only entrance or exit was the thin opening we'd gone through.

No no no!

I kept screaming hot breath into the man's hand. I hadn't escaped from my country and left everything behind just for this to happen the moment I landed. Tears pricked at my eyes, half fear and half anger.

"Calm down," he said, quieter now. Angrier. "What else were you going to do here? I'm trying to help you. You want to make money, don't you? All the pretty girls do." His sneer betrayed his jealousy.

I bit down on the flesh of his palm.

"Shit! Bitch!" He squeezed my cheeks painfully, my teeth cutting the inside of my mouth.

I whimpered involuntarily. The piercing pain screeched higher.

The bearded man had followed his friend, light-colored feathers curling off his clothes. He grinned wider at my pain. "Gotta teach you a lesson."

I was crying now.

"Let's show her what she's in for. Get her ready for the other customers." I didn't know which one said it, and I didn't care. Instead, my brother's voice rang through the high note of agony in my brain.

"It doesn't matter what it takes to get them off you."

"But if we're going to die anyway—"

He took my face gingerly in his hands to make me look at him. "Then we'll die fighting."

I wished he were here with me to fight by my side, but I did the next best thing. Determination flared through my body. I hurled myself up, narrowly missing the bearded man's gut as he shifted in time to dodge my kick.

A scream ripped from my throat as he barreled forward, intention in the assault.

"No!" I twisted and kicked but it wasn't good enough.

They both held me down, one from the front and one from the back, tugging and pinching until I couldn't move. The hand on my mouth pressed hard enough that I couldn't part my lips to bite or shout for help. My small movements couldn't stop them.

I thought I'd be safer here. It should have been safer.

My skirt was yanked up, then my undergarments down. Air touched me. I was naked and helpless. I could only look away, fighting for every breath. It was like I saw the whole thing from a distance.

But then, in the gap between the building and the wall, a shadow blocked the strip of sunlight. Another man here to join in? This person was huge, much taller than the others. I couldn't see much out of the corner of my blurry eye.

"What the fuck is this?" he demanded, glaring at us. His voice was low, hard-edged, used to being obeyed.

"Get out unless you want some!" spat the man with his hand over my mouth.

The new stranger chuckled. Chuckled. The sound was dark, threatening and self-assured. What did that mean? I couldn't imagine that was good. Who would laugh at seeing my predicament?

"Oh, I want something," he said. Then he moved forward with breathtaking speed and plucked the bearded man off me as if he weighed no more than a child. A punch sent him sprawling to the ground.

The man holding me let go and stood, fists clenched. I crawled away as fast as I could, fixing my dress. Again, I was stuck. The enormous stranger blocked my way out. I curled up in a corner, hugging my knees.

I finally got a good look at the newcomer as he faced off against my first attacker.

The fight was not fair.

The new man stood a head taller than the sailor. He looked younger too—maybe thirty—with golden skin and dark hair falling around his clean-shaven face. Despite the hot weather, he wore brown leather trousers and a loose shirt. The material couldn't hide his muscular chest and thick thighs. Sleeves reached down to his elbow. His forearms, veined and corded with muscle, were heavily scarred. Even his long fingers, not closed in a fist like his opponent's, had scrapes and callouses.

The sailor glared up. The newcomer looked down. As coiled as my attacker was, I couldn't believe he would win against this enemy with power emanating from every pore. His flashing eyes alternated between hatred and amusement. For a while, no one moved.

"Pay attention." That flashing, powerful gaze flicked to me, locking onto mine right before he burst into action.

2

VILET

My gut somersaulted.

Quicker than the eye, the new man lashed out at the sailor who'd attacked me. A kick. A punch. A crunch. And he was holding my attacker by his neck as he yowled in pain over his obviously broken leg.

"She didn't want to go with you," the man said simply.

"We didn't hurt her."

Another crunch. Another scream. "And I didn't kill you. There's more than one way to hurt. I know lots of them. Should I show you?"

The sailor was blubbering now.

"I think so." Again, the newcomer looked at me. "Do you think so?"

I didn't answer. I had no proof this new person didn't want me all to himself after this was over.

"Now, what I should do is twist off your prick," he continued, like someone else would recite chores to do.

The man went sickly pale.

"But you're not worth the extra seconds." He let my attacker fall as he released him. "Go. Leave, or I'll do it."

The man limped away, dragging himself as fast as he could go, cursing as he went.

The second attacker's body lay still beside me. He hadn't moved since he was tossed away.

My knees pressed against my chest as I panted with terror, holding myself close. The tall man turned his full focus on me. His attention lit up my body like heat. Even if I had been in a busy street, I doubt I could have looked at anything else. His power and confidence and beauty sucked everything toward him like a whirlpool. Despite my fear, I doubted this man would be as crass as the others. He might have an ulterior motive for helping me—probably did—but something in me wanted to trust him. Stupid thought. I was a bug being lured into a flashy predator's mouth.

After looking at me for a beat longer, he exhaled. "I should have twisted off his prick." He didn't come any closer, and my face relaxed.

"That would have been nice," I admitted. My voice didn't sound like my own. It was too much breath and rasp.

The stranger laughed again, this time louder. Then his amusement faded, the lines around his steely eyes deepening.

I couldn't quite get over how handsome he was. No, that wasn't the word. He was power and temptation, good and evil mixed. His mouth made me think things I shouldn't, especially after what I'd just gone through. What was wrong with me?

"Did they hurt you?"

Yes, but I knew what he was asking. "Not yet."

He ran a hand through his thick hair. The movement

showed off definition in his biceps even though he clearly wasn't trying. My stomach liquified at the sight. "Good," he said. His attention slid to the unconscious bearded man where he lay too close to me. Was he dead? I couldn't tell. "Or else," he continued, "I would have killed them both, slowly, in front of you, and enjoyed it."

Emotions surged through my blood at that. Part of me wanted to see it, wanted to see this huge, beautiful man taking pleasure in protecting me. It felt like a fantasy. Too good to be true. I bit my lip.

"You look like you just arrived," he said, more business-like now. Again, I knew instinctively that he was used to being followed, every order obeyed to the letter. "I did too. Can I walk you to where you're staying? Card isn't kind to women traveling alone."

I stood shakily to my feet. "I know."

The stranger backed out of the alley in three strides, freeing my way out. My feet itched to run, to hide, but somehow, being with this man felt safer than camping in the hills somewhere.

"What's your name?" I asked, as I emerged back into the light.

"Leander." A dimple appeared in one of his cheeks as he looked down at me. Up close, he was even broader, like a shelter I could winter under until storms passed.

"Vilet," I replied.

"Vilet." His sinful mouth caressed the syllables, but I still felt no threat toward me. He stayed close enough to discourage others to approach, but far enough that I had breathing room. "Where are you staying, Vilet?"

I wanted to live in his rich voice, like the baked sugar bread of my youth. But I couldn't answer his question. "I'm hungry," I hedged. "Let's get something to eat."

"A drink?" he guessed.

I nodded. The past few minutes were too much for me to process. I wanted to drown my pain, all the layers of it, until I lay in oblivious darkness. If I did it with Leander, I'd be safe.

I couldn't say why I felt so certain. He'd fought off my attackers, broken them, but I knew it was foolish to put my trust in someone so quickly. Vash might trust him if he were here, but the other person I'd left behind—my best friend, Yasmin—would bare her teeth skeptically and beg me to be careful. Hopefully, they were both okay.

I would be careful. And I wasn't lying. I did need something to eat. My stomach felt practically sunken in after four days without food.

Leander and I were silent as we wove our way out of the docks and up a stone path. From here, we could look down at the dock and the sea below. The Corae Strait looked like a blue jewel. I'd have to add that description to any letter I managed to send to Vash. He'd be impressed. The beauty of the land-scape and my companion distracted me from the protesting pain in my legs. The path twisted back and forth up the steep, rocky hillside. We hiked past another switchback and arrived at a building, asymmetrical to account for the slope, that had a wooden sign swinging on an iron hook outside: The Shell and Lemon.

"Tavern," Leander explained as we went in.

The front room wasn't full. It was an odd time of the after-noon to eat, so only a few stragglers bent over their mugs or bread or soup. They all looked up at Leander. No one spared a glance for me. That small mercy made me warm to Leander more. If he had to, I had no doubt that he could fight off this entire room of people. I glanced at his body again as he lowered himself into a chair. Every move he made was so masculine, so self-assured without being cocky. It was an earned pride. It made me wonder what else he could do with his hands...

"Some of the cults are vicious in Card," he said in an undertone, snapping me out of my thoughts. "It's gotten a lot better, believe it or not, but there are still assholes who only see people as currency. They can't drag people to the Eros-suna anymore, so they're getting creative. And it's not just them. Aphriso's fine but Card is a rough place. So, what are you doing here?"

"Visiting family," I lied.

He grunted, tipping his mouth.

"You don't believe me?"

"I'm used to being lied to. I've gotten good at spotting when someone's doing it."

I swallowed, my pulse hitching up again.

"You don't have to tell me." His inflection was so familiar. I thought I'd heard somewhere that citizens of Aphriso sounded like us. Maybe all the Eight Realms spoke the same, with no difference in accents.

The idea gave me a grain of comfort. Nothing in my speech would give me away. "What are *you* doing here?" I asked.

"Visiting family." His deep-set eyes gleamed. A muscle ticked in his jaw, daring me to call him out.

I stared at him, feeling bold, but ended up saying nothing.

"Town's a fucking mess," he said, calling over the innkeeper and ordering us two specials and two beers. "*Almost* makes me wish I were back home. I'm sorry you got caught up in everything."

"Can we not talk about it?"

When he returned my gaze again, I couldn't help but remember how he'd seen me exposed. Complicated feelings threaded through my chest. I'd left my undergarments in the alley and wore only a knee-length dress, soiled from the voyage despite my attempts to wash it off in the sea. At least I was still cleaner than I was an hour ago.

"Of course," he said. "I understand having things you don't want to relive." He placed one hand on the table, giving me a full view of his lithe fingers. "Let's not talk about any of it, any of our past. I like the idea that you don't know me at all."

"And I like the idea that you don't know me."

That dimple appeared again. "No past. All right. Future. Do you want something in the future?"

My eyes lowered to his mouth, then back up. But that idea was too dangerous, too reckless. Thinking became as difficult as wading through water with him around, all his magnetism presenting resistance. "To live a peaceful life." I shrugged.

"What does that mean?" The question didn't come out as someone else would have asked it. Behind the words there was bitterness and longing and true confusion, as if living in peace were a fairy tale he could never enter.

His reaction exposed my similar feelings. I didn't want to tell him what a peaceful life meant to me, what I fantasized about. I hadn't told anyone my secret dreams. Dreams were luxurious, expensive, and paid for in grief when they didn't come true. If I didn't speak them aloud, I was allowed to keep them. I shrugged again.

Leander's attention flickered around the room before he said, "I want to get away, find a small island where no one lives, and move there. No one would bother us. It would just be food and drink and talk and late nights under the stars. Maybe time with someone... special, whenever they come along. Or lots of special people, if they want to come." His smile was wicked, and a little unsure.

It was the first trace of uncertainty I'd seen in him, and gods, if it didn't draw me in more.

Bug.

Predator.

This was an honest piece of him. Judging from his commanding presence, he wasn't the type to talk about his fantasies very often. If we had been talking about armor instead of our hopes, he would look a lot like soldiers who came in for their outfitting. In build, anyway. The warmth in his eyes didn't match Ares' vicious warriors.

I gnawed my lip. He watched. My core grew molten. I squirmed a little in my dress. "I want ducks," I blurted.

This earned a hearty laugh. "Ducks?"

"Yes, and a pond far away from civilization. I'll learn to play the kithara and on summer nights, we'll catch fireflies." My voice caught. "My brother will live nearby with cattle. Every full moon we'll eat together—me, my brother, his family..." My voice trailed off.

Leander regarded me, dark eyes searching. "I want that for you."

"It's stupid." I brushed a rogue tear from my eye.

He caught my hand. Sparks ignited in my blood, licking up my entire arm. His rough hand engulfed mine in humid warmth. "It's not stupid at all."

Then, suddenly, he released me, as if he realized what kind of reaction I might have to being touched by a man again without being asked first.

"It's not stupid," he repeated. "Ducks are great."

"They are. With their little bills." Why did I feel so comfortable with Leander? His physique dripped violence. Those shoulders were brutal. Those pectoral muscles had been crafted with power in mind. I shouldn't let down my guard, but he coaxed me to relax like no one had in ages. He was a wall that could stop anyone from getting to me.

"Are you alone in this scenario?" he asked.

My skin zinged at the question. "No," I said carefully.

His lips twisted upward a fraction. "Let me guess. Duck wrangler? Bodyguard?"

A breathy laugh escaped my nose. "Exactly."

The food and drink arrived, smelling tangy and fishy. Leander and I tucked in without hesitation. We didn't talk until the food was gone and most of the beer consumed. Leander ate food efficiently, vigorously, just like he did everything else. Our relatively tender conversation seemed to break the norm for him. I would have bet all the money in my pocket that he'd never talked about how "ducks were great" before today.

The bubbles in the drink lightened my head immediately. "Why did you save me?"

I pressed my lips together. I hadn't meant to ask the question.

He looked up, dark eyes framed by dark brows. His gaze pinned me in place. "I wanted to do something good."

Disappointment settled in my middle. What had I expected? That he saw something magical in me?

He settled back in his chair and crossed his arms over his chest, almost contemplative. "I've done a lot of bad," he said, voice lowering, "and I'd rather do bad things to bad people. Those fuck-offs clearly deserved broken bones and you clearly deserved to watch."

My blood sang at the dominant undertones of his words, the confidence that he could overpower anyone if he merely decided to.

"Any half-decent person would have done the same," he said. "Problem is, there aren't many of those in Card. Honestly"—he leaned forward, crowding against the small table—"it was a pleasure."

His voice slid against my skin like gently scratching fingernails. I shivered. "I don't have a place to stay tonight."

Another admission. I shouldn't have had the drink. Damn it, *one* beer shouldn't have had this much effect on me.

Leander's eyes flamed. The intensity, the *invitation* in them made me cross my legs hard to tend to the ache there. "The tavern has rooms," he said.

My breathing had grown choppy. I thought I could feel his heat from here. Unless I was seeing things, his gaze settled, heavy and sultry as a touch, on my lips, my neck, my breasts. This huge, powerful being wanted me.

"Where are you staying?" I asked.

"Wherever you want me," came his quick response.

I could hardly hear over the blood pumping through my

chest. It wasn't even nightfall, but I needed to feel safe, to feel wanted, to be held, to have sex, right now.

My movements had grown clumsy. "There's probably a room here," I said, rising to find the person who had served us. I froze. Did Aphriso use the same money? I should have known the answer, but education came second to work or service in Eriset, so I had no idea if all the Eight Realms used the same currency.

A shadow rose behind me, dwarfing me within it. Fingers tenderly caressed my shoulder, then traced down my arm to my elbow, the touch impossibly light. It only made me want more.

"Is there..." I spun to face him. His chest met my eyes. I craned up. He was so big he could swallow me whole. "Do you... have a room?"

His eyebrows twitched in a sort of acknowledgment, as though he understood my true question. "I do now."

The next few seconds were a blur. Money exchanged, following someone down a hall, getting a key, door closing us in. When the door clicked shut, everything came back into focus.

Me and Leander. In a room. By ourselves. And he was looking at me with pure sin in his gaze.

He blinked. "You sure?" he asked, husky and ready.

I laid a hand on his bicep. It was hard and warm under my palm. "In the field," I said, "with the ducks, I want *this* with someone who can keep me safe." It was one of the last hidden pieces of my heart. Love was something I couldn't afford for so many reasons, but something my soul and body craved anyway.

"I'll make it good for you," he promised.

No one had offered that before. They took, whether it was like in the alley today or with men I chose back home. Their needs were more important than mine. I was a vehicle for their pleasure. My body could get them off, and, while I tried to reach climax myself, reach that place in me that yearned for release, I never crested that wave before my partner's savage thrusts turned into a grunt of pleasure and it was over. At best, they thanked me.

"Show me," I breathed.

❧ 3 ❧

VILET

This close to Leander, with his hard, capable body, my skin was on fire. I wanted him to command me. I'd obey. The thought made me so wet I felt a trail down the inside of my thigh.

A little bed sat tucked into the corner of the room. It wouldn't be big enough for him, for us, but he sat on it and drew me close between his legs. Our breath mingled as we leaned in. His big hand flattened against my back, almost covering it. I wanted him to scoop me up and hold me tight against him, fitting us together.

His full lips tipped up to meet mine, all heat and slow, careful hunger. He explored, tasted. I pressed open his lips with my tongue, leaning more heavily against him. His erection bulged against my seam. How had I caught the attention of this giant, beautiful man? I held him more tightly, crawled up so I was straddling him. Maybe if I held tightly enough, he wouldn't let me go. Maybe if I made him feel good, he'd keep protecting me. It was another one of the fantasies I was an expert at crafting, but I clung to it as viciously as I clung to him.

His massive hands swept down to cup my ass. He pulled me firmly up his lap as though I weighed nothing, settling me on top of the cock straining through his pants. It teased my sensitive places, and I couldn't help but grind lightly against him.

"Fuck," he breathed, breaking our kiss. His beautiful eyes were closed like he wanted to focus entirely on the place where our bodies ground together. Like it was ecstasy.

I watched him, spellbound, even as I found a rhythm. He rocked me against him, confirming he liked the tempo, his hands squeezing my butt, then relaxing.

My face flushed with heat, sweat breaking out on my skin. I saw the sheen of it on his neck too. Emboldened, I licked a long line from his throat up his chin. He tasted more delicious than the meal. When I did it again, his adam's apple bobbed under my tongue and I pressed us together more firmly. I wanted more. More friction, more touching, more skin. More *him*.

He had to feel how wet I was by now. My arousal had soaked through my dress, all along the thick length of him.

I hooked my fingers under the hem of his shirt and he helped to pull it off the rest of the way. His body stole my breath. Chiseled, strong lines that spoke of physical domination, but he was marred by wicked scars. They tore like lightning through the gorgeous flesh.

I gasped.

Leander gave a sardonic, rueful look. "Part of the job."

The pain lurking behind his eyes made me want to help him forget it all, everything that had disfigured his carved body, so he could drown in warm, piercing bliss right now. "No past," I murmured against his chest.

His rough hands pulled off my dress, leaving me completely exposed to him. I had scars too, though none to match his. My garment fell in a heap with his shirt. "Ooh," he growled, thumbing my nipple. "My beautiful girl."

He grew harder under me. Leander was commanding, in control, except for the slightest hitch of his breathing when I settled heavier on top of him and rocked. When he bit his generous lower lip, I felt my insides unraveling. All that pent-up energy, that fear, that tightly wound control were coming loose. I loved this, but the edges of my vision went red with alarm. This was wrong. I needed to keep that tight grip on control, otherwise terrible things would happen.

I clenched my thighs hard around him, trying to gain my bearings. He was the ocean and he was taking me under. That huge expanse of tan skin, those muscular arms wrapping around me now...

"What's wrong?" His quiet voice cut through my thoughts. I caught his eye through my lust-filled haze. His gaze bored into me, pupils flaring, but his hands stilled. Almost as if he knew I needed to pause.

No one had paused before. Not for me.

"What do you need?" he asked, deep, a sound that vibrated through my body.

"I don't..." *I don't want to lose control.* My recklessness—maybe some would call it bravery, but that felt generous—had allowed me to escape war-torn Eriset. Without a safe haven here in Aphriso, the only thing I had was control of my body. Could I let this stranger take that from me? Could I give it to him?

He smoothed hair away from my temple. He was so close. The heat of him, the clean desert-and-ocean scent of him, nearly drowned me. "We don't have to do this."

"No," I burst out.

His lips curved.

"No, I want this."

He shifted underneath me and the lump of his erection scraped a needy spot at my wet center. I stifled a moan. "How about this?" His velvet voice grew even softer. "If you want to stop, slap me twice."

"Slap you?" My face flared with so much heat my skin felt tight.

"Wherever you can reach." His smile was wickedness itself. "If you do that, I promise I'll stop. Let's practice."

My gut writhed with anticipation. "Okay." The word was a sigh, covered up by his mouth, swallowed by him, licked by his tongue.

I was drowning, and it was wonderful.

Blood pulsed, needy, between my legs as I wrapped my arms around him to hold him closer. His chest pressed against mine, every movement teasing my hard nipples.

I thrust my hips forward again, rubbing frantically against him. My wetness nearly embarrassed me, shouting the truth of how very turned on I was, of how I wanted him to free his cock and slide it inside me, of how I wanted to be touched until I couldn't bear it anymore.

"Slap slap," he grunted.

Dry-mouthed and blurry, I hit his broad back twice. At once, he stopped moving and separated our bodies, holding me lightly by the arms. Air chilled the newly burgeoning sweat on my chest. I felt petulant, deprived of his warmth and overwhelming masculinity.

"See?" he said, his mouth soft with lust. "Do that at any time and I'll get off you. I'll stop what I'm doing."

My brain hardly registered the words that came after *I'll get off you*. Which meant he'd be *on* me.

I nodded.

He smirked and kissed me. No, it wasn't a kiss exactly. He tasted my bottom lip. "I want you to feel safe with me. Two slaps, right?"

I nodded again.

"Now," he said, "what do you want?"

"This," I breathed.

"No." He spoke like a teacher, or maybe a friend. Impatience welled inside me. "Tell me what you want me to do."

Then I understood. He was giving me power—power to stop, power to go. He still felt like an unstoppable wave, someone who could make me forget my own name if he wanted to, but he handed some of that natural dominance back to me. I swallowed, strangely touched, but I didn't know how to answer. Commanding a lover was utterly foreign to me. I hardly knew what I wanted, except for him to make me feel good, and for me to do the same.

"Give me an example," I whispered.

He cocked his head, the faint light from a lantern (which I

hadn't noticed until then) played along the fierce, beautiful line of his jaw.

"For example," he began slowly, "I could tell you to get on your knees and suck my dick until it goes down your throat."

His eyes glittered. It was a dare, not a command.

I slid off his muscular thighs until my knees hit the ground. I didn't break eye contact until I needed to undo the clasp of his trousers. He spread his knees so I could fit more comfortably between them. My fingers felt numb as I clumsily wrestled with the buttons pressed taut by his bulging cock. Finally, the last one flicked free.

I raised my eyes to his again. Leander watched me hungrily, fascinated. I stared back, feeling his crotch blindly, reaching beneath his underwear to pull out his length. A vein pulsed under my palm. He was so hard already. I squeezed and pumped my hand up and down, earning an unholy noise from Leander. He leaned back on his hands, bracing himself to watch me.

My fingers met around his cock, but he felt too stiff and heavy to go down my throat. The very idea sent a new ache between my legs, though. I'd try.

I started with a tentative lick to the head before slurping the tip. Again, but harder, my cheeks sucking in. His thighs trembled. His pleasure was headier than the beer. I could drink it until I burst. And I felt like I would. My ache was cresting to unbearable levels.

Holding onto him with one hand to guide him into my mouth, I pressed two fingers to myself with the other, rubbing to alleviate the desire pooling there. My own pleasure coupled with his as I sucked him harder, deeper, almost made me come. He tasted salty. I traced the stiff lines of his cock with my tongue as I pressed in.

"Down the throat, my love."

His words were measured, calm, but I could tell from his body how much effort it took him to sound so composed. He sat up, abs rippling, and threaded his fingers through my hair. He held my head in place, taking the lead now, thrusting up into my mouth. I could do nothing but hold on. His legs flexed with thick muscle as he shoved his hips up.

Then he slowed. His next thrust was slow, deliberate, intense. I was choking on him, balls deep, as he slid down my throat. Even the hand at my own center stilled to make space for his body, the head as I swallowed him. I could hardly breathe. I thought of the two slaps needed to make him stop, but my body felt suspended.

I gasped as he pulled out, my saliva dripping from his erect cock. That was one of the sexiest moments of my life.

Leander's breathing sounded as ragged as my own. He hauled me onto his lap again, smoothing spit from my lips with his thumb. Somehow, he looked bleary and intense at the same time.

"Your turn."

I racked my mind for what to say. "I want..." I couldn't think. There was nothing but his body and his breath and the memory of him in my mouth.

"Tell me."

"I want... you."

"Be specific. *Tell* me."

My desires sounded filthy in my head, something to *do*, not talk about, certainly not something to demand from someone who looked like a muscle-bound god. I drew in a breath. Leander gazed levelly at me, waiting for orders. Summoning courage, I straightened and lifted my chin. "Rub my clit and fuck me at the same time."

"That's my girl."

I was in his arms, grabbed, pinned under him, my back on the bed. The thin mattress bounced with the speed of his movements. He ripped his pants down the rest of the way and flung them with the rest of our clothes.

"See, you could do it," he murmured, sucking a kiss from my mouth. I suspected he liked tasting himself on me. "Keep telling me what to do, what's good for you. Yell at me, move me, whatever you have to do, all right?" With a growl, he kissed me again.

He ran his big hands down the full length of me, catching on my breasts, running down my ribs and over my hips. Those hands felt so strong and capable that it wasn't surprising when he found my clit right away with his thumb, rubbing in relentless circles. His body had been honed into something deadly and accurate. He knew his own body and knew his way around other people's. I squirmed against his hand and new fingers joined the first, searching through my swollen folds, slipping through the wetness, gliding inside. His touch was brutal, demanding my surrender. A cry built in my throat, rising higher and higher. He didn't let up, only repeated what made me tremble and tense and writhe.

I squawked, an indelicate sound, but when I opened my eyes, Leander only gave a burning, cruel smile. He knew what he was doing to me, that I was coming undone.

"Come," he said. "Come on my fingers."

He didn't wait for my response. He demanded it. He wrung it out of me with quick pulses and friction, so much friction. I couldn't withstand him if I tried. My core squeezed, wet and fire-bright, as I cried out, finding my release. He kept rubbing, kept pulsing his fingers inside me to ride it out. When my orgasm subsided to a bearable level, I found Leander still playing with my center, but almost playfully now. Slick and aching, I drenched his long fingers, but his expression quelled any shame I might have felt for letting myself go so entirely like that.

"That's it," he soothed, settling himself between my open legs. His ready cock pulsed with veins. "You said do both at the same time?"

"Yes." I shook my head and realized how sweaty my forehead was. In that moment, I knew I wanted to see Leander as sweaty as I was. His golden skin looked flushed, but I wanted him wet, straining under the pain-pleasure of sex. I wanted him needy, cursing and saying my name. I wanted the power of seeing him lose all control.

He nudged my entrance, teasing. From this angle, he towered over me, even though he sat on his heels. The entire landscape of his curves and ridges looked like a place I wanted to get lost. Ropy scars slashed ruthlessly across his body.

I tried to scoot forward, to impale myself on him, but he stopped me. One calloused hand rested on my knee while the other hovered near the place we were almost joined.

"You said both."

He fingered me, rubbing, immediately building up that ache again. My interior muscles flexed around nothing.

Then, something.

He eased himself inside me, deeper, filling me, stretching my walls. I was so slick from coming on his fingers that he only felt good.

"Oh gods," he breathed. "You're so warm. You're so wet." His hand and hips moved in time with his words.

I gasped.

"That? Yes?"

He thrust in small, sensual movements, like a dance to show off his beauty, while his hand did its expert work. A whimper escaped me. No one had ever done something like this for me before. Here, I was queen, even while he completely dominated me.

When I caught my breath enough to speak, I said, "More. Harder. Lose yourself."

He obeyed, driving deeper with punishing strokes. Even as his speed increased, he never took his thumb away from my clit. He could wring pleasure from me like water from cloth.

I tightened myself around him and he released a breathy sound, something between a gasp and a laugh. "So tight. Do that again."

I did.

He groaned. His thrusts became more desperate. The muscles in his neck strained, every part of him flexed.

"Yes," I encouraged.

He grunted, "Gods..." Now he was gripping my hip with his free hand, anchoring himself as he pulsed into me. His thumb flicked wildly.

I panted, leaning into that throbbing ache. I was close, close.

His balls beat against me with every deep thrust. He was

feral now, chasing his own release. The concentration on his face as he pushed in made me melt, opening new spaces for him to press into.

A faint voice told me to slap him twice. Could he pass that test? Did I really have as much power as he claimed?

But I couldn't bring myself to do it, not with my own orgasm so close.

"Lie down," I ordered instead. I wanted to feel his whole body straining against me. I needed the friction of his groin and his chest and his flat stomach.

Twitching with the pulses of pleasure that threatened to take me down, I reached out for his arm. He understood after a second and hurled himself down, catching his body on his elbows. One hand immediately snaked between us and kept attending to that aching bead at my core.

Over his shoulder, I saw his ass as it flexed. His wounded back moved like a wave.

I whimpered. He moaned, panting, indecent.

We yearned, finding something together. We were reaching. We were letting go. We were gripping so hard our nails broke skin.

I shattered into a scream, fluttering and shuddering around him.

A bead of his sweat dripped into my open mouth. I tasted the salt and musk of him.

"I'm—"

He couldn't get more words out. Every muscle in his abdomen grew hard. I felt each one. Then his hand left my clit and he gripped himself as he came out, pumping fast. His heavy breathing was half grunt, half sigh. A surge of heat splashed across my belly.

In the silence of that hot room, our panting was the only sound. My thundering heart began to slow until I didn't feel it batter against my breastbone anymore.

Leander angled up. He glistened with sweat. A satisfied smirk crossed his sinful lips. He was still breathing hard, chest rising and falling in time with mine. "Vilet..." A wide smile tugged at his mouth, creasing the corners. It was happy and sloppy and I wanted to hold the image in my mind forever.

"That was good," I murmured. My stomach bore obvious evidence of what we'd done, but I didn't wipe it off.

Did mind-blowing sex mean we'd ever do it again? It was probably best not to. The idea left me bereft. Because that hadn't just been achingly good sex, it had been a glimpse into what power could be if it were used for good instead of for violence. Leander protected me, and then made sure I felt comfortable in bed. All that didn't stop him from being brutally efficient in getting me off. I wanted so much more of him. But I had no idea how to ask—or even whether I should.

"Stay with me?" I asked.

He raised a dark brow at my question. I'd meant it as another command, but the lifted note at the end betrayed me.

His face fell.

My gut did too. I sat up and propped my back against the headboard.

"I can't," he sighed.

I didn't know what to say. I still didn't have a place to stay the night, unless he let me keep this room.

I nodded. "That's all right."

"I wish I could." He shook his head. "*Gods*, I wish I could."

"Is..." A sudden thought caught me by the throat. "Is someone waiting for you?"

"No," he said quickly. "Nothing like that. I have to be somewhere, and I'm not staying long in Card." He laid a heavy hand on the inside of my thigh where I'd crossed my legs, but the touch wasn't sexual this time. He soothed the sensitive skin with his thumb. "Just a few more days and then I ship out."

Ship out. I didn't like the terminology. It sounded warlike. He bore himself like a soldier. Was he a soldier in Cytherea's army? Did Cytherea even have an army? What a foolish idea—all gods and goddesses did.

It was probably better that he was leaving. What was I thinking to instantly become involved with a stranger? Leander's leaving would make it easier for me not to stay in Card and to get on with the mission of finding someplace quiet and surviving.

"It was very good," he echoed, his palm smoothing down to my knee. He grew serious. "Will you be all right?"

"Fine."

"Will you?" Lantern light played in his dark eyes, as though a fire raged within.

"Yes."

"*Will you?*"

I slapped his corded forearm twice.

His expression melted in understanding, but he stopped pressing me about it. The truth was, I didn't know. I wanted to be all right. I suspected I never would be. Not after growing up in the shadow of fear, not after leaving everything I knew behind, not after... this, whatever *this* was.

"I'm required in less than an hour," he muttered finally, but he scooped me into his lap and held me there, his scars pressed to my side. He dwarfed me, enveloping me in muscle and warmth.

In minutes, he would leave. But for now, I felt safe.

Sometimes, now had to be enough.

❧ 4 ❧
VILET

I pushed past crowds, keeping my head low. No one told me today would be some kind of celebration. But apparently everyone from Card wanted to carouse in the streets this morning.

Excitement coursed through the hordes of people. It kept laughter pitching high and drink flowing as servers exchanged cups for coins as they wove through the crowd. The evident anticipation only served to spike my nerves.

When I woke up alone in The Shell and Lemon, the sheets still smelling like Leander, I resolved to leave. I'd hike into the mountains and find a smaller town, somewhere safer, and settle down. Once I found my feet, I'd discover a way to reach out to Vash and Yasmin, if she was willing to leave her family, and bring them here too.

It was a simple plan. I liked it. The problem was actually making that happen.

For the journey, I needed a few supplies like food. With

hardly any money, that meant I'd have to trade work for goods for a few days before I could leave.

And that would be a whole lot easier if every cranny wasn't bursting with bodies of workers and partiers and tourists. They had to be tourists. Every style and look was represented by the chattering people streaming past me. Was Leander among this crowd? Was he taking part in these festivities?

I wracked my mind for any holidays I knew Aphriso celebrated. There were a few, but none happening today that I was aware of. To be honest, I couldn't be sure what day it was. The darkness of the ship's hold only allowed me to guess how much time had passed.

"Behold!" someone shouted.

No, I wasn't imagining it—the crowd got thicker here. So many bodies pressed together that I couldn't walk any further. I tried to wedge between two men, gritting my teeth at the feel of a stranger's arm against mine, but they only gazed down at me with irritation for a moment. Instantly, their eyes returned to the object of everybody's attention. What was everyone looking at? Even though the crowd around me was clearly human, not deathless, they were still tall enough to block most of my view.

Bouncing on the balls of my feet, I finally saw what the speaker was talking about. A large puppet theatre, rising to the same height as the portly announcer, had been erected in the square.

"The time is fifty years past!" cried the man, wearing a fashionable white leather suit. Delicate white protrusions burst from the end of his sleeves like dandelion fluff. He gestured grandly to the little stage. "This is a story of tragedy, of resilience, of lost loves."

Puppets crowded onto the little stage, hanging from complicated wires. Each figure represented a man or woman against the background of a port city clearly meant to represent Card. The figures appeared to chat together and sell their wares.

"It was no ordinary day." The announcer stretched his arm wide. "For the sun would soon cease to shine! The darkness of the Eclipse would mean darkness upon all the people."

I frowned. Normally the Eclipse was celebrated positively. It was a time of great power, so, although some people felt apprehensive, it was usually a time to let loose and revel with others.

"As the unsuspecting citizens of Queen Cytherea's fair island went about their work, everything was about to change," the announcer continued.

The puppets all turned in the same direction and began to tremble, their painted faces grotesque in the sunlight.

The announcer brought his wide hand over the sun to shadow the stage. The puppets' trembling doubled.

"A rumble. And then another. It was a sound like thunder at first, nothing to worry about."

A child whimpered near the front row.

"But then the thunder became a roar! As if the very ground beneath their feet would split. And it did. A chunk of this very kingdom—blessed by the goddess—broke off and crashed into the sea, taking with it many lives."

Three puppets hurled backward out of sight.

I grimaced. This was awful. I finally understood that this

was a reenactment of the great earthquake. In Eriset, it had been one tragedy of many, remarkable enough that people talked about it, but not as shattering for us as it had been for other places, apparently. No part of Eriset crashed into the Corae Sea.

"In the darkness, the ground shook as if Typhon himself picked us up to rattle our bones." The announcer mimicked the action as he spoke, sending the white feather decorations bobbing.

"The quake jarred all Eight Realms. There goes Menos and Nalia, Kantharos and Zenia, our fair Aphriso, then Hyperion and Eriset, rumbling across the Stygian Sea all the way to the Far Realm!"

Murmuring and gasps took the crowd.

The announcer obviously reveled in his audience's reaction. "Oh, it was hard. Hard even after the quaking finally stopped and we were left to see the damage."

The set of the portable theatre now looked rent into two pieces. A puppet cried. I raised a brow in disgust. If this were a made-up tragedy, I wouldn't mind—my neighborhood was fond of legends and fairy tales—but dramatizing something so horrible? I glanced around. A couple people looked old enough to remember what happened.

"The casualties," the announcer continued relentlessly, "the carnage, the broken pieces, and the dead!"

The child in the front row was really crying now.

"It was a day to remember." The man's voice quieted. He peered solemnly at the ground. "But we have risen stronger than ever before, rebuilt with the leadership, the guidance, the beauty, and the strength of one deathless deity."

My heart seized. The announcer rotated to look behind the stage. Even the puppeteers stood so that the tops of their heads were visible. All of them focused on the raised platform cast in shadow under a large roof. I hadn't noticed it before in the white-bright sun. There were *thrones* underneath the shelter. There was no other word for them. One was larger, white, with what looked from here like velvet and pearls and feathers. The other was austere by comparison but no less regal. It was made of black metal with blood-red cushions on the seat and backrest.

Priestesses, marked with piercings visible through the diaphanous material they wore, marched from the wings toward the thrones, pouring out drink offerings. They stood as one, chanting blessings upon the goddess, Queen Cytherea.

Ice surged through my gut. It couldn't be. *She* couldn't be here. The coincidence was too great. But that white throne looked made for her, from everything I'd heard.

Then... who was the other throne for?

Panic threatened to blacken my vision. The only reasons I knew a lot about three particular gods were that two battled for my land, and one of those was having an open affair with Cytherea.

The queen appeared near the sheltered area and gracefully strode toward her throne. Her beauty stole the attention of everyone in the crowd. At least, I assumed so, based on the way everyone went so silent. Cytherea looked as soft and ruthless as the sea, dressed all in white. Her dress draped artfully to leave large swaths of flawless skin exposed. Her long hair formed a thick braid like a crown around her head. Her every movement was sensuous, inviting.

If not for the deathless male marching next to her, I wouldn't have been able to tear my gaze away.

He wore brown leather armor and red body paint smeared over the thick cords of muscle on his bare arms. His hair had been shorn close to his head. His violent smirk verged on insane. With the slight adjustment of his sculpted lips, it looked like he could go from predatory and amused to terrifyingly intense in an instant.

My heart froze as my tormentor's vicious gaze swept over the crowd. Although this land was Cytherea's, I had no doubt he saw it as his own. That look of arrogant possession said it all.

Did he see me? Did he know everything? Nothing seemed impossible. If he caught me, would he pull me apart and drink my blood to make a point?

The things I'd heard and seen growing up returned to me in a sickening wave. I'd never seen King Ares in person.

But there he was.

Both he and his twin sister had ferocious reputations, but Ares outstripped Bellona in sheer cruelty. He *liked* blood. He *liked* pain. Humans were playthings to him.

My vision threatened to blacken at the edges.

Around me, people clapped. I followed their lead with numb hands. I couldn't be the only one abstaining from applause. Ares would see. He would pluck me up like a fish from the water, happy to have caught something to feed his bloodlust. I got off my tiptoes, letting the people in front of me block my view.

The announcer spoke again. "We humble ourselves before you, Cytherea, goddess of passion, queen of beauty. And we welcome the mighty King Ares, god of war, to our Day of Remembrance celebration."

Hearing him say the name made me stiffen even further. I chanced a look around. Even more had joined the festivities. No way to escape. Even if I could edge my way out of the crowd, that movement would surely catch his attention.

Guards and attendants flanked the two deities once they stood before their thrones. Cytherea's attendants were beautiful, topless. Each had creamy smooth skin with a couple strategically placed piercings on their navel, their cheek, their collarbone. Back home, nudity wasn't common. The dangerous and harsh conditions necessitated that we cover up. Seeing so many bare chests, both male and female, fascinated me for a moment.

Ares had guards too. Tall, silent, standing behind him in shadow. Had any of them come into the shop while I was working? When I scanned them, my breath caught as surely as if a hand had reached around my throat and squeezed.

Leander.

Leander was one of Ares' guards.

I knew his shape instantly, despite the dimness underneath the shadowy roof. He became clearer and clearer the longer I stared, my eyes adjusting.

And he was looking right back at me.

✿ *5* ✿

LEANDER

The meat in front of me tasted like ashes, but I forced myself to chew. This was the last place I wanted to be. It didn't matter that our quarters had golden silverware provided by Queen Cytherea herself. The ale and stew with Vilet had tasted twenty times better.

Vilet herself tasted twenty times better.

Nothing less than Ares himself could have torn me away from holding her in my arms. It felt like I'd known her far longer than a day. I didn't know her history, but we were exactly what we needed in the present. Gods, that mouth, the trusting way she'd looked at me...

I couldn't let my mind wander. I chanced a glance at Lord Ares and straightened my spine. He sat at the head of the table, two people away from me, so the soldiers didn't act as rowdy as they normally would. The king only sat with his warriors in the field or on trips like this. He drank pomegranate juice with such relish I wondered if he mistook it for blood.

Someone to my left passed a dish of oysters. I took one without thinking and passed them on.

"Hey!" Achos pushed the dish back. "You know I don't eat those after a trip."

I'd forgotten. Probably because I thought Achos' superstitions were stupid, but we were all at least a little superstitious. Hard not to be when the slightest thing could mean the difference between life and death. At the beginning and end of every week, I scraped a layer off the inside of my leather uniform, right under Ares' spear emblem. I'd done it so many times that the spear was hollow. I had to be careful now not to let any of the damage show, but the ritual still happened without fail. After all, I was alive, wasn't I?

Ares observed our interaction. Most of the time, when he observed something, he did it with the blankest look on his face, as if his eyes wouldn't focus. It was when his eyes widened and fixed on something that you knew you were in trouble.

"More!" he suddenly shouted, gesturing to his final bite of goat topped with goat butter.

A flash of creamy skin meant someone was moving. I looked above the heads of the soldiers eating their meal to the line of topless servants sent from Cytherea. The tightness in their faces showed how uncomfortable our presence made them. I'd have been uncomfortable too, unarmed and bare like that with Ares. I changed out of my light shirt and back into my leathers as soon as I returned to the palace. The other time I came to Card with his entourage, Ares made us watch as he choked one of the servants. The other soldiers laughed. All I could manage was to relax my face so I looked amused. I hated myself for it afterward.

I'd seen a bit of that woman in Vilet when we first locked eyes. She was in trouble, but I was finally in a position to do what I'd wanted to do so badly that other time.

Yesterday, when I'd gotten half a day off after we landed in Aphriso—Ares wanted to be with Cytherea alone—I didn't expect anything beyond a deep breath. Maybe a drink and a walk to clear my mind. I didn't expect Vilet.

The most fucked up thing was how I still felt a little loyalty to the god of war. How could I not? He'd saved me from the streets. I was strong enough to defend myself now, and then some, because of him.

I was five when Ares found me. I was skinny and dirty, living alone on the streets, picking peels out of trash heaps. His soldier gave me an entire loaf of bread to make me go with him.

I had no parents. Demi-gods weren't always paternal. Sometimes they were simply monsters, like my father. Didn't stop him from copulating, though. Last time I checked, I had twenty-seven half-siblings, and that was a low estimate. Obviously, my father (a dragon-shaped demi-god) and my mother (a human prostitute who died of disease about a month before Ares' soldier found me) weren't able to give me a home. Loving homes were a nice myth in Eriset. The reality was strength, battle, and survival.

Even now, despite the fact I was fully grown, fed on meat and wine, the crackle of crusty bread could set my heart racing. It meant life to me.

I didn't realize it meant death too.

Training for Ares' army almost killed me. Many times.

When I was twelve, I considered escaping.

By the time I was thirteen, I knew I never could.

Careful not to let Ares see my jaw flex with frustration, I took another bite. It had been ages since I really *talked* to someone. The others would mock me for even thinking that. We were all doers, not talkers. But it had felt so good to banter with Vilet, even though I had to sidestep who I really was. She was honest and earnest. And we'd brought each other to the best kind of sweaty relief. Vilet had been more than a good portside lay. Much more. She was a cautious dreamer, like I wanted to be.

Could I really keep going like I always had now that I knew what a different life could be like?

Ares picked up the knife he used to carve his meat. His eyes fell on me.

My skin pulsed with alarm.

He twisted the point under his fingernail, rotating it slowly as if to make it catch the light. None of the other warriors made a sound now.

Had I done something to displease him? Had he noticed how distracted I was? I didn't let any worry show on my face. Instead, I simply waited for him to speak.

"You're going to the ceremony tomorrow. Choose two others."

A game. He must have felt relaxed. But games were dangerous too.

I scanned the warriors along the big table. "Lys and Gegenes."

"Why not Achos?"

I didn't look at the soldier in the seat next to me, but I could feel him stiffen and his breath hold.

I answered honestly. "Lys and Genenes are the strongest, and Achos fought with Lys on the voyage here. They might distract each other."

Ares' manic gaze slid from me to the space over my shoulder. I didn't move. "Fought?" he asked.

"Yes, my lord."

He was drawing this out too long. Normally, our only warning was a look in his eye, and it was all over. We scrubbed pieces of our comrades off the floor when he was done. But now? We knew it was coming.

His chest expanded in a deep breath as if drinking in our fear. I sent up a silent, useless prayer to the Divine for the servant not to return now.

"Fighting, fucking... it's good for the blood!" he declared.

I took a small breath. Was he really not going to kill Achos? Did the prospect of a night with Cytherea distract him that much?

But then a smile curved Ares' pomegranate-stained lips.

Achos jerked. He didn't scream. None of us did when we were in pain. Some of the drills we suffered didn't make us stronger at all. They just hurt.

But this wasn't like the drills. The soldier writhed, his hands twitching to his uniform. The metal clasps. The rivets. Ares was torturing him, driving them into his skin by the look of it. Yes, there was the blood.

Ares, completely at ease, let out a chuffed laugh.

I hated him. Rage filled me from my feet to my hair, but I didn't change my expression.

Achos' noises increased from erratic breathing to grunts and squeaks, but he clamped his lips together and didn't beg for mercy. Civilians begged. Ares' army never did.

The king's power gave one last heave and Achos slumped over his oyster-free plate. Just a demi-god. Killable.

Like me.

Maybe I deserved death more than Achos. As horrible as it was to sit next to a corpse, I couldn't help but wonder if my position was really any better.

THE NEXT DAY, I FITTED ON MY LEATHER ARMOR. THE metal fasteners felt cool against my skin, but I knew they'd get hot in the sun. Little rivets were better than the metal-plating we wore when the weather wasn't as sweltering, but the reminder of what had happened to Achos at dinner didn't improve my mood.

That could just as easily have been me, impaled to death. I'd made myself valuable enough as a tracker that Ares' attention usually ricocheted off me when he wanted to unleash his violence, but still.

I got off easier than many. Only scars. But my body was nearly disfigured and some of them took months to heal.

"It's good," the others said. "Toughens you up."

I fit the last clasp and straightened.

I wasn't afraid of hard work. I wasn't afraid to kill or be

killed at need. But I didn't want the torture of serving Ares to last my whole godsdamn life.

It was almost a shame I was so fucking good at what I did. Otherwise, I'd have more distance from the one who made my life hell. Ares kept me in his personal rotation of guards, which meant the options were to serve or die a painful death. In my mind, the options were almost even.

Too bad there wasn't another choice. Maybe all life was hell —I didn't know. I just made the most of what I had to deal with. Talking with Vilet, though, made me wish I was the person she thought I was. She didn't look at my scars and recoil because they were proof of my allegiance to a violent deity. She touched them gently, with an unspoken promise to make me forget whatever had happened. She thought I was kind.

Shaking off the memory, I strode from the room, sheathing a knife at my hip as I went. Lys and Gegenes were waiting in a small, bubbled room at the end of interconnecting hallways. I didn't like how white everything was. I felt like I would break the feathery decorations just by standing near them. Red accents—jewels and shimmering paint—looked like blood on snow.

I scanned the guards going with me. They wore the right attire and weapons. I knew better than to pick a fight with either of them, but I didn't enjoy their company either. Gegenes was a demi-god too, but he had a specialized power. He could grow another pair of arms out of his torso. It was fucking creepy, but it made him an almost unbeatable fighter. Lys was... disturbing. Maybe that was the best way to put it. He had a power too—

temporary madness. As in, Lys himself was always on the verge of it, with spittle regularly coating the corners of his mouth, but he could also send madness into animals. Make them rabid. And then there was me. I was one of the unlucky ones who had to depend on universal powers and my own hard-fought training.

"Lord Ares waits for us," I said.

Lys licked white spit from his lips. "It's just a spectacle," he grumbled.

"A ceremony. And you will treat this as seriously as any other exercise." I paced down the white hall on the opposite end from where I'd emerged, knowing they'd follow. Sure enough, light footfalls echoed my own.

The hallway opened out into the main area of the palace with high ceilings and even more breakable decorations and insecure openings. I noted them. Part of tracking wasn't just following clues after something happened, but noticing details beforehand.

In the center of the room stood King Ares and Queen Cytherea, with a few of her servants. Cytherea's legendary beauty drew my eyes, but I immediately looked away. Hopefully Lys and Gegenes were smart enough to do the same and not linger on her exposed white skin. We'd already lost one guard on this trip.

"I've lifted the wards," Cytherea said.

That meant we'd all travel through the air. Good. That would make things simpler.

Ares growled in his throat, as if she'd offered to suck his cock. He was even more unpredictable when he was with Cytherea. I'd witnessed firsthand how the smallest look or movement could set him off. Apparently, his time with her yesterday hadn't made enough of a difference.

"I'll go first," I said. "Your majesties can follow. Lys and Gegenes will go with you."

"Go." Ares dismissed me with the wave of a hand.

I bowed my head and stepped into the blackness between spaces. On my walk yesterday, I'd scoped out the ceremony area so I knew where to go. Whether or not Lys and Gegenes knew didn't matter, as long as they followed the residual divine power.

In a blink, I landed on hot stone pavement a few steps away from the covered platform where Cytherea and Ares were supposed to sit while somebody performed rites or made speeches. The others materialized right behind me. I stiffened involuntarily at the nearness of people who would kill me without a second thought, and that included Cytherea. A lifetime of practice kept my body from showing its reactions.

"The casualties!" someone cried. "The carnage, the broken pieces, and the dead!" His theatrical voice, rising above the muted sounds of a crowd just on the other side of the cypress trees, made it clear he wasn't shedding any tears for the casualties he talked about.

Cytherea's topless servants slid between our bodies to enter before the rest of us, as I'd been told would happen. The sight of their perfect breasts marred only with a single piercing awakened only the ashes of desire in me. Lys leered openly at them. It made me want to smash him in the jaw, do to him what I'd done to those sailors in the alley. No, I didn't want these servants, who never spoke or acted outside the will of the goddess. If I had a choice, which I didn't, I would choose

Vilet. Her skin had flaws. Having sex with me had made her both bold and nervous at first. She was real. She was brave.

I swallowed, gazing ahead at the opening where the god and goddess would emerge.

"But we have risen stronger than ever before," the announcer continued, "rebuilt with the leadership, the guidance, the beauty, and the strength of one deathless deity."

Ares and Cytherea moved into position. At a glance, no threat to them lurked behind us. If I had to protect Ares today, it could only be from the crowd gathered to see them. I followed the couple through the cypress trees to the covered stage.

Cytherea's servants chanted something softly as she maneuvered to her throne. Ares' sat right beside it. I took my place behind his seat, made completely of dark metal. He must have requested that. My throat constricted to think of what he could do with that. I should have been used to thoughts like those by now, but they rose up and choked me at unexpected times. Now wasn't a good moment to hate Ares.

Focus. I looked out at the mostly human crowd gathered in the square. The announcer we'd heard stood between them and us, wearing the stupidest outfit I'd ever seen. And there were puppets. *Divine help me.*

A head of dark hair bobbed up to see between taller bodies. My skin, already heated from the sun, went ice-cold.

Vilet. That was Vilet. She looked back at me from the crowd facing Ares. Why was she here? Fear turned her eyes to perfect circles.

I stiffened, every muscle remembering what it felt like to

be with her. She didn't belong in my brutal world, and a bolt of pure apprehension ran through me. *Run!* I wanted to shout, but I couldn't. I couldn't show that I knew her. Ares was already acting volatile on this trip. I couldn't point her out, couldn't reveal how much it would hurt me to see her damaged.

But I could tell from the terror on her face that I'd already damaged her by being here. By being what I was. Unlike others in the mass of people who seemed nervously curious, Vilet was petrified. I knew that look. She came from Eriset. She knew what Ares could do.

Then what was she doing here in Aphriso? I should have sensed she was from Eriset. Her reluctance to talk about her past, even her voice should have given it away. It was barely different than people spoke who were native to Aphriso, but it was an accent I was so used to hearing that the truth hadn't fully registered.

She ducked out of sight.

The ridiculous announcer was still blathering on about the holiday as Ares cast Cytherea a savage, possessive look. She gave a half-smile in response. Neither of them listened to the presentation either.

It was good that Vilet had disappeared. She'd go somewhere far from here. I'd never tell Ares she was here. All the circumstances told me she had fled from Eriset—the War Twins would see that action as desertion, treachery, but I couldn't blame her. I couldn't blame her for that horrified expression, either, when she saw who I worked for. That didn't mean her terror didn't kick me in the gut, though.

When I met new people, their default reaction was fear.

And rightly. Ares' army saved me from the streets, but it brutalized my soul, if I still had one.

I missed Vilet's face already. She had Eriset coloring with sharp eyes and a small, tough frame. Small enough to hold. For the first time I could remember, with her I felt... heroic was too strong a word... maybe kind? She didn't know the atrocities I'd witnessed, or those I'd done. She only knew that I helped her and then we had heart-pounding sex. It couldn't last, but I enjoyed pretending to be the hero for a couple hours. *No past*, she'd said.

I fucking wish.

I tightened the grip on my knife hilt, trying to pry Vilet from my mind, but the harder I tried, the more she clung on. Ducks. She said she wanted ducks. Her vision of a peaceful life stirred something in my chest, and now I couldn't get comfortable. Ducks and cattle and a remote island would haunt my dreams and probably distract me at the wrong moment someday. Peace, with Vilet, was the most intoxicating idea I'd had in decades.

It wasn't just the curves I took in handfuls or the wet sounds her pussy made when I rubbed it, it was the false hope she embodied. More painful than a knife thrust. Hope made one weak. But she'd given it to me anyway.

I couldn't see her anymore, but the crowd flexed around an invisible object moving north. It had to be Vilet.

Good. Run. She didn't want me now anyway.

Ares surveyed the crowd. Hopefully, he wouldn't murder here for his own amusement. He kept his maniac outbursts to Eriset, for the most part.

As I stood, muscles flexed, ready to assist the god I hated

more with every minute, my eyes returned to the place I'd locked eyes with Vilet.

Hope was cruel. I tried shaking it off, but it wouldn't let go. Instead, my mind churned out more silly ideas, half-formed plans of what if, what if, what if...?

We were off Eriset, in a new kingdom. There might not be a better opportunity for me to get free. Stupid thought. Ares would track me down and kill me. Was that worse than this life, though? If I got to spend a week with Vilet, pretending not to be a monster, wouldn't it be worth it?

Leave was never planned. Ares or one of his other generals would wave his hand, tell me when to be back, and that was that. I didn't want to wait another second to be unleashed from Ares' side.

Maybe I was no better than my father, a demi-god lusting after humans, but this felt different. Deeper. Being with Vilet connected me to a completely different part of myself. With her, I didn't have to act like a weapon that condoned violence for its own sake. Ridiculous as it sounded, I could dream with her. Good dreams, not nightmares.

Even though I stood here wearing armor and holding a knife, Vilet was the brave one. She was right to run from Eriset. If all we had was that one hour in bed, I was grateful for it. Because it knocked something loose in me.

Vilet represented a chance. And I was going to take it.

❧ 6 ❧

VILET

Tears stung my eyes as I fought through the crowd. I'd felt *safe* with Leander. I was an idiot. Of course he was deathless. Of course he worked for my enemy. From the moment he appeared in the alley, I should have known simply from the ruthless efficiency of his violence.

I wanted to cry, but I needed to run.

Leander could draw attention to me in the crowd. I couldn't have that. The throng around me was so huge, everyone straining to get a glimpse of Ares and Cytherea, that I could move farther away, out of sight, simply by ducking down and moving deeper into the crush. I needed to go in the opposite direction eventually, toward the hills, but for now, hiding was more important.

Why did Leander have to work for Ares? The betrayal slashed like a knife.

Don't come after me. Don't come after me. The nonsensical idea that Leander would swoop down off the platform and drag me back wouldn't stop circulating in my thoughts. Every touch of a body or an arm as I squeezed past made my belly clench. One of these touches would be Leander's, my mind kept insisting.

My breathing sounded unnaturally loud. The announcer was still saying something, but at this point I didn't care. My reality had contracted to a tunnel of taller bodies and the piercing ache of fear and betrayal.

Through the crowd, then out of sight. That was my plan. I couldn't think further ahead. Ducking lower, I turned to see if I could make out anyone following me. Apart from the weird looks I got by pushing past people, nobody seemed to be stalking me. Not Leander and definitely not Ares. The reaction he'd get from this crowd would give him away in an instant.

That didn't mean I felt comfortable. All the deathless could appear and disappear at will. Were they toying with me? Was Leander whispering in his ear right now, telling him what he suspected about me?

I didn't even tell him I was from Eriset. Maybe he doesn't know. Ares' soldiers weren't omniscient. It just felt like it sometimes.

Finally, the number of people thinned and the crowd couldn't offer protection anymore. Another glance behind showed the covered area with the thrones as a small square in the distance. No chance I could see facial expressions from here. No way to know if Leander was still looking at me.

If I thought a knife or club would do any good against Leander—or, Divine forbid, Ares himself—I'd have grabbed one. No, my only hope was in secrecy. I hadn't done a great job of that so far with all my suspicious behavior, peering around and barreling through the crowd. Stopping behind a building for a second, I gathered my thoughts.

I'd run until I couldn't anymore and then hunker down in the woods somewhere and hope Ares' army would "ship out", as Leander put it. It wasn't a bad plan.

You didn't tell him where you were from. You said nothing about working at an armory. Ares is here for the holiday and that's all.

Waves of calm alternated with waves of panic as I put my plan into action.

Staying in the shadow of the buildings, I slowly weaved away from the water, toward the hills. Escaping Eriset had been grueling. I refused to be retaken now because I made the bullheaded mistake of sleeping with one of his guards.

I rolled my eyes as I ran. How could I have been so stupid? Was I so lonely that the first beautiful male I saw turned me to jelly?

I thought I was stronger than that. I thought I was smarter than that.

With a deep inhale, I reached the tree line. There weren't enough trees to hide me until I got further in. Although my life had been about survival, I didn't know much about living in the wilderness alone. Would there be wolves or other mountain beasts? Demi-gods were sometimes born in the form of some unlikely creature. Were any of those around here?

The steep hillside, smelling of salt and sweet sap, pitched up above the port and lower buildings. From here, cypress trees hid the stage from view, but the crowd was so big it was still visible through the trees.

Not far enough.

I'd only had one cup of water that morning at The Shell

and Lemon. Almost no water for the entire voyage over the Corae Strait plus the strenuous activities I'd foolishly chosen with Leander made me parched now. My heart jogged in my chest as I kept going.

Just keep moving. Panting, I reached the top of the rise. It was a false summit. The hills and valleys leading to the rocky cliffs of the mountains kept rolling on. I picked up a fallen branch as an excuse to slow for a moment. It had a jagged edge. Not exactly a spear—Ares' symbol, so, a fitting weapon —but it would do. It was all I had for now, anyway.

The sounds of talking faded to a muted buzz. Birdsong was louder. That was a good sign. Vash taught me that complete silence usually meant a predator was near.

Lightened, I reduced my pace but didn't stop walking until my legs threatened to give out sometime in the late afternoon. I'd resorted to using the spear-stick as a walking prop.

I was exhausted and thirsty and weak, but I hadn't seen a soul. Maybe Ares' forces wouldn't come after me today. Maybe I really had made it to safer ground.

Here. I could stay here for a couple days until I was sure that Ares and his entourage were gone. There was a large tree on a steep hillside, with roots that formed an opening that faced downhill at a diagonal. The hollow looked big enough for me. I could cover myself in leaf litter and peer out.

Once I tested out the spot and snuggled in, I had nothing to do but wait. Only squirrels and birds appeared, flitting from tree to tree. No monsters or animal-like demi-gods in this part of the woods. For now, at least. I'd seen a couple in Eriset near my home, so they were probably in Aphriso too. Yasmin swore she saw a blue-skinned one with bulging eyes and huge fangs sitting near the water one time. The one I saw last year was just a buzzard with human arms. Unnerving, but a lot smaller and less intimidating than others I'd heard of. Since demi-gods weren't full deities, they couldn't shift back into a human shape. A horrible fate. Compared to that, I'd almost rather accept my human self. We had puny little lifespans, though, as the deathless constantly reminded us. And inflicted upon us.

Despite my practice with waiting and staying silent until danger passed, this time felt different. Thoughts of demi-gods brought back the image of one in particular. My mind was just the tinkle and crash of breaking glass. Fragile hope tipped over and threatened to shatter.

I wasn't safe yet.

I'd managed to escape, ready to set up a new existence far from danger where I could provide a good life for my brother one day. I'd felt secure for the first time in years when Leander cradled me against him.

Hope.

Seeing him standing with Ares himself... Leander wasn't just a soldier in the Twin Armies—he was clearly a high-ranking member. Ruthless. Bloodthirsty.

No past. My ass. He probably said that to everybody just so they wouldn't run screaming. He had years and years of practice lying to people. Maybe he pleasured others the same way too, just to see what it felt like to be anonymous. He probably got off on it.

My throat tightened.

I hated who he was, how he'd lied to me, how he was no different than the other evil strangers I'd met.

I had no right to miss him as much as I did.

The thing was, talking to him yesterday was easy. He would fit in with Vash and Yasmin, like some big, sexy bodyguard.

The forest darkened slowly as I watched. Swallowing a tough lump in my throat, I scolded myself for thinking that way, but daydreams kept floating before my half-focused eyes.

Yasmin's gaze would dart to me over a meal of smashed potatoes. *My gods,* that sparkling look would say, *where did you find this guy?*

Vash's stern face would thaw as he talked with Leander, growing more convinced he actually cared about me.

They'd both ask hard questions either to him (very carefully) or behind his back. We'd become fast friends. Leander would guide me to bed that night and make love to me until I was trembling.

A chilly breeze cooled the tears on my cheeks. I wanted Vash and Yasmin near me as much as I wanted my next breath. That was all it was—marrow-deep guilt and loneliness. Not longing. Definitely not longing for a soldier of Ares.

❧ 7 ❧

LEANDER

Back at Cytherea's palace—the pointy, frosty, feminine, white cake of a castle that made me feel like a hulking brute every time I visited—I stood at my post. Unfortunately, I was posted outside the queen's royal suite. People would notice if I left.

When I left. Because I was going to escape. No better time than here on Aphriso.

The pounding and screaming inside the room grew louder. My stomach roiled. They'd been at this for hours. The queen's reputation for loving sex wasn't an exaggeration. Even sex with Ares, who wouldn't take her pleasure into account. His focus, in every moment I'd interacted with him, had been himself. His own gratification. What the stunning queen saw in him, I didn't know. Maybe she was selfish too. Something about his power, maybe...?

I shook off the disgusting thoughts. Ares caught a lot of people in his web. I shouldn't judge. For a while, I'd worshipped him too, devoted myself totally to the cause. Until

68

I saw that it didn't matter what I did, he'd never care about me. He'd never see *me*. Even if I won his war for him.

Didn't mean I had to like the animalistic noises coming from Cytherea's chamber, though. They grated on my nerves and sent images of Vilet rushing back.

My cock down her throat.

Her simple request as she lay sprawled beneath me.

Sitting with her at that table talking about ducks, of all things.

I squared my jaw, trying to tune out the shrieks and growls. Tonight. I'd leave tonight. After seeing Vilet's expression in the crowd, I very much doubted she'd want to flee with me, but I'd try anyway. My skill in tracking was the thing that made Ares notice me first and assign me to his personal guard. When I found her, I'd explain everything. She could hate me if she wanted to, but she deserved to know the truth first, that I hadn't meant to hurt her and that I hated Ares too.

I scoffed under my breath. I was a ruthless warrior in Ares' army who secretly longed for peace, if peace existed. Not much to recommend me to a resilient woman who had every right to be afraid.

Gegenes swung open the door on the far end of the room, passing the ethereal clouds of naked attendants. "Sentinel, message for Ares," he grunted, thrusting a paper into my hand.

I didn't look at it. "He's not accepting messages." Gegenes knew that. He had this same guard assignment a couple days ago.

"Give it to him when he's done."

I almost said *he's never done,* but I bit back the comment. "I'll give it to him."

Gegenes left without another word. Cytherea's attendants dotted the room, jumpy at the presence of the god of war and his soldiers. They moved swiftly out of Gegenes' way. I would too if I were them. Did any of them know about the extra arms? It didn't matter, really. Violence followed Ares wherever he went, and demi-gods were no exception. Demi-gods were only immortal until they were killed.

Ares always insisted on bringing his own guards—not relying on Cytherea's, for instance—because we wouldn't hesitate to kill on his behalf. I wasn't proud of it, but that was true of me too.

I unfolded the paper and glanced at it. No seal meant this wasn't classified information.

Evidence of a stowaway discovered on grain ship bound for Card, Aphriso, from a SE port in Eriset. Investigation has concluded with reasonable certainty the stowaway to be a 22-year-old human woman named Vilet, worker at the 7th armory of Lord Ares, who abandoned her post in the glorious war. No remains have been found matching her description, leading us to believe she lives.

Vilet (pronounced vill-ETT, her employer told us) is short and slight, with light skin, dark hair just past the shoulders, and knowledge of metals and heat. She has a scar behind one ear and another across her torso, with burn scars on several fingers. Likely at large in Aphriso. If found, return her to Eriset so she can stand at her post. If she does not go willingly, her usefulness to the cause has ended.

"Wine!" Ares demanded through the door.

I jumped.

Quick as a whisper, Cytherea's guards disappeared to obey.

I crumpled the note in my hand. Vilet. A stowaway. This

explained everything except how I was going to stop Ares from hearing about her escape.

Damn it—Gegenes knew everything. He loved a hunt. He'd tell others, and...

I blinked. Cytherea's servants had left to get the wine. Leaving me alone.

My ribcage seemed to tighten. Imagining this moment was one thing, but now that I had the opportunity to run, could I? I'd seen many times what Ares did to deserters. He didn't just kill them. "Bringing Vilet back to her post" was bullshit. If they found her, they'd eviscerate her if some overzealous bastard didn't finish her quickly. The same would happen to me, and worse. I was Ares' guard. Working at some armory didn't make Vilet a soldier, but guarding Ares for years, growing up around him, would add personal betrayal to my list of sins if I went. Years of built-up reflex shouted at me to stay. Don't run. Don't be a coward.

But this wasn't cowardice. This was the first fucking sign of bravery I'd shown in a long time.

Vilet needed me. And fuck if I didn't need her. Life with Ares wasn't life at all, and now I finally had a clear shot at the door. If Vilet didn't want me, fine. I'd understand. But I'd help her one way or another.

Time to find out if peace was real.

❈ 8 ❈
VILET

I knew what nighttime footsteps meant.

At best, they were the furtive movements of friendly people coming to deliver a warning.

At worst, they meant blood was seconds away.

Here in Aphriso, I knew no one. I curled up into the pile of leaf mold under the great tree roots, holding my breath. Lack of air and light to see had me imagining things. Stars glowed like fireflies in front of my eyes.

The footsteps grew closer. Stopped. No other sounds pierced the quiet.

The slosh of the pulse in my ears was maddening. I couldn't hear, couldn't see, couldn't breathe. And someone was coming.

If I didn't move, the person would pass. Right? I'd been in enough heart-stopping situations that I knew the pounding of my pulse wouldn't alert most people to my presence. It was a myth. One that my traitorous mind wouldn't believe. *It's loud! You'll be caught!* it said.

I huddled lower.

A shuffle of leaves. "Vilet," came a whisper. Then a hand over my mouth. "Don't scream."

My body twisted around in the darkness, manipulated until I stood beside my sheltering tree, my back pressed against a hard chest. I couldn't stifle a whimper as I writhed in his arms. Escape was impossible. His body was like metal.

I knew that body. Humiliation joined the terror jogging through my limbs. It was Leander, the one I'd thought was safe.

Nowhere is safe.

"Vilet, it's me!"

My panic warped his words.

"I won't hurt you."

I scoffed against his rough palm.

"I know you're running from Ares. That's impossible unless you have help."

Now he was just insulting me. I bit his finger. Hard.

Hissing in a breath, he spun me around. Faint moonlight peeked above the hollow, revealing the murky outline of his face and the harsh intensity of his gaze.

He was going to kill me. I thought of Vash, who wouldn't know what had happened to me, who had said, *Then we'll die fighting.*

I kneed Leander as hard as I could in the groin. He grunted, but his grip on my arms only tightened. I couldn't yank them away. Fear winded me, but Leander seemed merely frustrated.

"Just listen!" he said. "Stop trying to fight me. You'll get yourself hurt."

I kept thrashing. He kept holding me tighter. His arms barred my upper and lower back. His strong body cocooned me. Everything was him. To keep moving started to feel... intimate, so I slowed. When I did, I finally remembered something.

Slap slap.

When I hit him twice, Leander released me and stepped back. I let out a shaky breath, not sure my legs would hold me up.

"Shit," he hissed. "I shouldn't have scared you."

"You're a soldier in King Ares' army," I spat back. For some reason, the accusation dripped with emotion. Leander hadn't personally betrayed me, not really. I never asked.

The lines of his body stiffened. "Yes. And we need to run."

I barked a laugh. "We?"

"Ares knows you're gone, or at least his soldiers do, and he won't be far behind. So yes, we."

My face went bone-cold. "He's coming here?" In the darkness? Where I stood in the chill with skin that might as well be paper for how it would hold up against the god of war? All deathless could walk through the air, disappearing in one place and appearing in another. I was dead.

My voice nearly failed. "You brought him here?"

"No," he whispered quickly. "Not intentionally. But I left. He won't be happy when he finds out."

"Wait, you're just walking away?" That sounded ridiculous. No one left Ares' army, not that I'd ever heard. Unless they died, that was.

"I don't want to serve him anymore." Leander's voice went quiet too. "I want to try the life we talked about in the tavern."

My mouth fell open. "That was dreaming. That wasn't real." A rock choked me as I realized I never believed my own words.

To survive. That was what I wanted. Peace was for other people. I wanted to believe in it, but all hope had wrung out of me.

"We can't run," I said. "Ares will kill me. You're still his soldier."

"I'm not."

"I saw you on the platform."

"I'm not."

My eyes adjusted further, and I took in his furrowed brow, his tense muscles. His deep-set eyes that willed me to believe him. My stupid body remembered his, and my face and pussy grew hot and achy. Good thing the night hid my blush.

We had a one-night stand—that was all—and I just needed to survive that mistake.

I shook my head. Leander was a soldier, through and through. How I didn't see it just showed how blind I was, how needy for someone to care. "Did you tell him about me?" *Please no. Please no...*

"No," he said, speaking lower though I could still hear. "I said nothing. But a letter arrived for him explaining your situation so we could all be on the lookout. I destroyed it, but that doesn't matter. People know."

I bit my lip, throat constricting painfully. My mind threatened to go white with terror.

His gaze dropped to my mouth. "After yesterday, it just confirmed what I'd been thinking for a long time. I thought we had something, so I wanted to find you and see if we could run together. You are running, aren't you? From him?"

I didn't answer. My skin hummed with the feeling this was a trap. But his words were buttery. The pulse at my center kicked up.

The air grew thick and charged between us. The night smelled like pine. He felt it too, that same feeling we'd had last night. I saw it in the way our breathing was heavy and humid, in the way we didn't look away from each other, even though danger was coming.

Damn damn damn.

"I'm just an excuse for you?" My answer didn't come out the way I wanted it too. Damn, it sounded like I wanted him to run *for me.*

Leander squared his stance, just slightly, but enough to make me tense. "I hate it there. I hate what he's made me. You just gave me an idea to run toward." He relaxed a little. "Hopefully, you could guess this, but I don't often run."

"Idea..." I murmured, unable to fully comprehend that Leander was here. Here. And offering to—what?—protect me?

"Let's go," he said gently.

"No." My entire body trembled. "I need to go alone." But I didn't want to go alone. I wanted the protection Leander was offering—I just couldn't accept it from him. Ares' army was evil, no matter what Leander said.

"You need to not die." He lowered his head in warning.

"He'll come after you."

"He's already coming after you!"

"You left," I spat, every shadow in the corners of my vision waving like an enemy ready to attack. "Go do what you want. We are nothing to each other. We're strangers!"

"I want to help you."

"And I'm saying I don't want that."

"Vilet..."

I left my stick, which seemed so measly now, and began to walk away.

He grabbed my arm, twisting me to face him. "Alone will get you killed!" he hissed.

I squirmed, close to tears. He of all people should know better than to grab my arm like that. Alarm passed through his features, as if he realized the same thing, but he didn't let go. Instead, he stared into my face, close enough that his breath clouded against my mouth.

I was so screwed up. I shouldn't want his other hand to scoop me up so I could straddle his hard body. I shouldn't want his mouth on mine. But lust didn't listen to reason. Lust said, *Remember how safe you felt as he thrust into you? Remember his salty cock down your throat? Remember the things he murmured against your body as he let you take control?*

And here he was again, gripping my arm with those strong fingers, staring into my face with a mixture of alarm and concern. Willing me to hear his warning. Leaning closer than he needed to until the warmth of his face glowed over mine.

What did I have to lose?

His face stayed close, angry, waiting, and I kissed him. Attacked him, more like. I scrambled against him, grunting as I tried to get closer.

He lifted me like I wanted him to so we could reach each

other's mouths more easily. And he *wanted* my mouth. His tongue met mine as we kissed, deep and wet.

He walked us to the hollow, which formed a kind of wall, and pressed his weight between my thighs. I whimpered as he found a firm, grinding rhythm.

Oh, he was good. My breath hitched. He was demanding this time.

Demanding...

Taking.

I hit him twice on the back, where I was holding on for dear life. He ground deep against me one more time before he deflated, shoulders slumping, and backed away to allow my feet to find the ground. He heaved deep, needy breaths. A question peeked dimly through the arousal in his eyes.

"I can't... trust you," I said, trying to keep my voice steady but sounding exactly like a woman pulled out of lover's bed.

"What can I do?" His voice was raw. Something more than a short tryst with me lay behind it. Maybe he really was telling the truth about wanting to leave Ares for a long time.

I dismissed the thought. No one left Ares and survived. Hopefully, maybe, I was unimportant enough that I could get away with it.

"How can I prove I'm not on his side?" he asked. "You don't have to come with me—I can tell you where to go, what to do to give yourself the best chance—but you have to believe me."

Why did he care? I was no one. I tensed before I answered, "I can't, Leander. But I hope you do find peace. Go find your beach somewhere. I'll find mine."

He didn't get angry. He didn't attack. But he didn't walk away. "Tell me what to do."

"Leander…"

"Tell me."

The forest was dead silent. Maybe Ares would appear to track us down. There was no place nearby to hide. Was it worth it to linger?

The way he gave the command reminded me—reminded both of us, I was sure—of yesterday. My heartbeat thrashed again. Why could Leander play me like a fiddle when I didn't trust his intentions? A soldier, current or not, was dangerous.

"Get on your knees." I'd thought the words, but didn't realized I'd said them until he obeyed. *Oh my gods, what am I doing?*

"Hands behind your back." My voice came out small but clear.

He did it.

Oh my gods, oh my gods… I was so turned on, I couldn't sift through my thoughts anymore. Here was kind Leander, the one who'd saved me, who'd given me a way to feel safe even as we devoured each other.

Would he follow through when *all* the power and pleasure were mine?

I rolled words over in my head. They sounded absurd. This muscular demi-god wouldn't obey my sexual commands.

My next order was so outrageous, I couldn't say it to the whole forest. I had to whisper it into his ear. "Suck me. Make me cum."

He wasted no time trundling forward on his knees. I raised my skirt and he rooted his face into the sopping apex of my thighs. I gasped. He hummed, delight at a good meal, and flicked his tongue over the most sensitive parts.

Shit! My brain was piercing desire and curse words. I braced myself on his arms, still clasped behind him. I wouldn't be able to stay standing for long like this. He sucked and rubbed and licked until my belly was convulsing. I dripped into his mouth. I even had to clap a hand over my own to stop the moans from keening too high, too loud. When he growled, the vibrations sent my entire body shaking.

Oh my GODS! He was *working* with his tongue, but not just his tongue. I couldn't see everything down there—I'd dropped the skirt—but his lips and nose and teeth were involved too. He was relentless.

I took care not to double-tap his back.

The first orgasm barreled down the length of my entire body in violent shudders. He lapped up the evidence. The second almost made me cry out. At the third, I was starting to hurt, so I told him to stop.

Three times. He was definitely a demi-god.

My legs were shaking when he backed up, so I slumped to the ground.

"You're fucking delicious," he said, standing awkwardly for someone usually so agile. "Not being able to see... You know how to test someone."

That hadn't been part of my thought process at all. If I'd even had thoughts beyond how beautiful his body was and how I wanted him to be truthful. This encounter was a fairy tale right before the gory part. Another moment to hold off the inevitable and pretend together.

His crotch bulged, but he stood a pace away, not coming closer. I still couldn't catch my breath. The forest breeze played across the sweat on my face and neck. A tiny smirk curved his lips as he towered above me. He wore a knife at his waist, on the same side as the spear symbol on his chest. How had I not noticed either one before now?

Slowly, reality fell back into place.

I had to decide. To go with Leander or to go alone...

My body decided it wanted more of Leander, but I was made of more than primal urges. This decision could be the difference between life and death.

I peered up at him. He looked so capable up there. Well, of course he was capable—that was what earned him a coveted spot near Ares in the army. The question wasn't if he *could* protect me. It was if he *would* if the choice came down to me or his lifelong loyalty to an evil war god.

"I want to believe you," I admitted.

"Trust me, I could suck you all day."

His answer made a laugh burst out of me. "No, I want to believe you about everything else."

"You should," he said earnestly. "I... I'm sorry I'm not what you thought, but I'm your best chance right now."

If Ares really was coming here, I would be safer betting on Leander than trying to escape alone. Maybe I'd regret agreeing to flee together.

But what if I don't regret it?

The possibility of real safety was too big to count on. But I longed for it ferociously.

Leander licked his shining lips. "Time to make a decision,"

he said, only a hint of a smile on his face. Damn it. He knew how good that was for me. I couldn't deny it.

My brother said we should fight for ourselves. Well, I was about to take a bigger risk than getting on that ship leaving Eriset.

I was going to trust Leander.

9
VILET

Despite the underbrush, our walk through the forest was silent. The loud ones always got caught. We'd made enough of a ruckus in the hollow.

The fact of *Ares himself* possibly coming to find me and punish Leander wouldn't fully register. There was nothing to do but hike further away to a better hiding spot.

I made my steps small. For some reason, I felt awkward now. Small. Well, next to Leander, I was small. He acted a little stiff, and I could guess the reason.

What were we now? Allies? We weren't friends. "Lovers" was a stretch.

We were a one-night stand gone wrong. Refugees banding together.

Moonlight showed us just enough of the trail. Or maybe Leander had cat vision in the dark. Demi-gods usually had some extra ability. I looked at his profile but couldn't tell—his eyes didn't glow like a cat's or anything. He clearly saw better than I did, though.

"Oof!" I hurled forward. A root caught the top of my foot and the hard-packed ground jutted up to slam against me.

A hard grip on my bicep stopped my fall. Leander set me back on my feet. "You all right?"

The low question sent our first encounter shivering back. "Yes."

He released my arm. Maybe it was my imagination, but there was military precision in everything he did now. Catching me, even executing orders. *Suck me. Make me cum.*

Now that our awkward silence had cracked, I added, "You're a demi-god, aren't you?"

He raised his eyebrows in a way that meant yes.

"Could you take us farther away without walking? I mean..." I shrugged.

"Traveling? Sure, but it leaves a trail. Trackers can sense that kind of divine magic."

That was too bad. It would be interesting to disappear and then appear somewhere else. "Do you have any other gifts?"

For a second, he didn't answer. Maybe he hadn't heard me, since I was whispering so quietly. "No," he finally said, his tone laced with bitterness.

Had someone made him feel like less because of that? "Me neither," I said.

He looked at me, confusion giving way to that dimple. "I was counting on you to turn into a battle ax."

"Haven't been able to do that since I was nine. Sorry."

In just a few more steps, some of the chill between us had already returned. The truth of who we were was just too big to settle into comfortably. There was none of the ease we'd felt in the tavern when we could just *be*.

My mind was a jumble by the time we finally reached... somewhere. It was tough to see in the dark and I was breathless from hiking so long, mostly uphill. There were boulders and trees, maybe a gap that could be a cave near my feet. No, a crevice?

"Here," said Leander, halting and gesturing toward that opening.

"In there?" I asked, pointing to the black shadow between boulders that could harbor some monster—we didn't know. I didn't love the dark, and it was already midnight out here without creeping into a hole. "I don't think so..." Two people would not fit, especially when one was as big as Leander.

"It's the best place for now. You're not... Are you afraid?" He had no expression I could see. A cloud had blown across the moon, sending shivers down my back.

I stiffened. "No." It was the standard answer. In Eriset, no one admitted to being afraid. We couldn't afford to bring each other down, to make the fear real. It would suck us down like a whirlpool if we didn't get down to the business of surviving— getting food, finding good shelter, sensing signs of the next nearby attack and avoiding it.

"Then yes. Here is good."

I eyed the hole again. Leander could muscle that boulder right on top of me if I squirmed down in there.

He wouldn't, though.

Don't trust him. Don't trust him.

He gestured with that thick, glorious arm. The one he'd held behind his back because I'd asked him to, just to prove he was on my side.

I sighed and wormed my way in. Inside was a pocket of

warm air. No snakes or worse creatures. It was bigger than it looked from the outside, still black as ink, and still tiny for two bodies. My stomach flipped over. How could I think with Leander pressed up against me the rest of the night?

"Push to the back," he said. Soil gritted under feet and the opening grew even darker. He was wedging himself inside, facing outward.

I scooched away as far as I could.

Once inside, he heaved a breath heavy enough that his back touched my front. "Vilet... I'm starting to wonder if I made the right choice, bringing you into this," he murmured.

"It is tight."

"No, the situation." He didn't go on.

A few heartbeats passed. Then I lightly touched his back. "I wasn't safe before you, either," I whispered.

He was so close, blocking my only path to escape, but also shielding me from everything outside. It was almost poetically perfect to describe our relationship.

"Where do you want to go?" He didn't roll over to face me. Maybe he wouldn't all night. The idea left me disappointed.

"Just away from here."

"No, really. We should figure it out."

I blinked my blind eyes. He was serious.

"What about the Far Realm?" Leander suggested. "He won't go there." *He* was Ares. *She* was his sister Bellona. Leander and I spoke the same language.

"The Far Realm?" I hissed back. "Are you crazy?" We sent our dead—when we could afford the two-coin toll—to the Far Realm. Only dead-bearing boats could survive the wild Stygian Sea separating Eriset from the unknown. We hoped our loved ones had a good home, but the Far Realm was home to monsters and evil gods too. Stories about that place chilled my bones. It wasn't somewhere to visit.

"If we could find a ship from Nalia to take us...?" Leander pressed.

They did have the best sailors. Supernaturally good. Better than humans. But that would mean going back to the docks to search for something that wasn't there. Even if we did magically find a ship from Nalia, the Far Realm couldn't be an option. Could it?

"Doesn't King Hades still rule there?" I asked.

A sharp scuffling and Leander lay on his other side. I couldn't see his face, but I could feel his breath. My own grew short. I wanted him to tuck me against him like he did in the tavern. But there was no space to move. "We would have to go through Hades," he mused.

Rumors said that Lord Hades, god of the dead, scared even Ares—the only being who did. "Maybe there's... somewhere else," I breathed.

Wherever we went, it had to be somewhere Vash and Yasmin could go too. If we fled to the Beyond or crossed the perilous seas to find uncharted lands, they'd never find us. My heart sank.

"Would he follow you to Menos?" I asked. The name conjured a haunted fairyland from childhood stories, but it had to be better than here.

"Yes."

We lay in silence for a few minutes.

"I don't want to go back," I whispered into the dark.

"I figured that out when you fled the country and were willing to travel with me."

My lips twisted, but it wasn't quite a smile. "Why don't *you*? You seemed important up there. You were allowed to stand next to both of them." Ares and Cytherea. "And you're a fighter, obviously." I couldn't keep the resentment out of my tone. The very thing that made his body so irresistible was what made it so hateful too. Those hard muscles, those ropy scars, that physical confidence to get rid of enemies...

My stupid mouth went dry with want.

He sighed, and I felt it on my forehead. "Fighting for Ares isn't like what happened in the alley. It has no purpose. He just likes blood and victory, and for a while, I did too. I didn't know anything else." Was that shame in his voice? Today had broken something in him, it seemed.

Why was he admitting his love of violence to me? People I knew regularly fell victim to Ares' love of "blood and victory", as he put it. His confession wouldn't make me like him more.

"You saw the scars," he murmured. "Training for his army."

I blinked in surprise. It was already so dark that the difference didn't register. "You got those scars *training*? Not in a battle?"

"Most of them, yes. Ares is ruthless."

I laughed, my pain bursting out before I could stop it. "Tell me more about that. About how Ares is ruthless. You worked for him. There's some respect there, or tolerance, at least. I've never seen that..." I wanted to berate him with stories of what I'd witnessed, what I'd experienced, but we never talked about those things. The humans in Eriset war zones didn't need to talk about them. We were all there together. If I never told one person some of the horrors I'd lived through, it wouldn't surprise me. Better not to let those images live.

My purpose bubbled up again.

Peace.

Getting *away* from there.

"I wasn't trying to tell you something you didn't know," Leander said awkwardly. "I was just explaining."

Claustrophobia washed over me, drowning me in a smothering wave. Leander blocked my way out. Why was this happening now? Normally, I liked tight spaces because that meant I'd be harder to find. They were hugs. This wasn't.

I tried to force air into my lungs. "Get out, please," I gasped. "I need to breathe."

"What?"

But I couldn't explain. My vision sparkled with white stars. This space was tiny. Leander was huge. If we touched, I thought I would die. I'd have no space left...

My body jerked, flexed, trying to find space. Air. Life.

Tears started at my eyes and a whimper escaped my mouth. Maybe it sounded pathetic, but at that moment, I didn't care. I needed to breathe.

Now.

"Please." It was a wheezy whisper.

Finally, he moved, scooching out toward the opening. Moonlight looked bright after the total darkness. I grabbed my way desperately out of the hole.

My limbs were shaking, my back hitching with urgent breaths.

My eyes burned. This panic hurt, but the shame of not being able to stay in our hiding place hurt too. Panic was a liability. My head was a swirl of horrible emotions—fear, anger, shame, and I just needed to *breathe!*

When I finally started to catch my breath, body still trembling, I remembered Leander was there. He hadn't touched me or spoken through my episode. Instead, he sat near me with a concerned crease between his brows.

When I met his eyes, he exhaled. "I shouldn't have made you hide there."

I couldn't respond. I had been through hell my whole life. I was supposed to be as tough as Leander. It didn't matter that he was a demi-god soldier and I was a human.

"Sit up slowly. Breathe." He made no move toward me.

I did what he said. Cool night air began to fill my lungs the way it should. Dirt gritted against my bare ankles when I crossed my legs. Slowly, in pieces, the forest fell back into place around me.

"I'm sorry." Leander's low voice cut through my still-fuzzy consciousness.

"For what?" I asked hoarsely.

"Everything."

We lapsed into silence. Strangely, his words soothed me, like a bath when we had warm water back home. I'd needed to hear that.

I wiped my eyes. "Time to find a beach?" I barely managed the light tone I was going for. The words were too filled with the dark memories still hanging in the air like mist.

"Ducks?" he returned.

My face relaxed as I looked up at him. It was the face that had appeared behind that building—the impossibly beautiful face that came to save me. Now, he felt more like an ally than a savior. Still painfully masculine and gorgeous, though. Maybe we wouldn't survive the wrath of the war god, but we had a dream. What was the harm in pursuing it?

His eyebrows darted down and he stood, fast and silent. My abs clenched, ready to respond. Ready to run.

He peered into the darkness. I hadn't heard anything, couldn't see anything, but I listened with all my might.

I could tell by the tightening of his thick muscles that we were definitely in trouble.

Where to escape...?

But before I could formulate a plan, someone burst through the air between us.

❧ 10 ❧

LEANDER

Gegenes stood between me and Vilet, coiled to strike. Ares had sent one of the best.

I acted automatically. He barked only half my name before my knife was out of its sheath at my waist. At the same moment, his extra arms extended through slits in his uniform, reaching for me. Not reaching for Vilet. It was only fucking luck that he appeared facing me instead of her.

Two brutal slices later, he lay with one hand detached and his neck gaping. The three remaining arms sprawled like a spider's.

I felt nothing but adrenaline. None of Ares' soldiers were friends. Friendship meant attachment. Attachment meant weakness.

Behind where Gegenes had stood was only empty space. My belly clenched. Where was Vilet? She should have been behind him.

Without the ability to walk through the air, there was only

one option. She must have fled, silent as a forest creature. No scream.

I chased after her.

My long legs allowed me to catch up with her easily. She was mine to protect, so small against the forces that followed us now. Barely a shadow beneath the trees.

Ares never sent just one. Vilet knew it too, by the way she was running, narrowly missing tree trunks as they rose out of the darkness. The pine needles barely shifted under her feet as she sprinted away.

I cursed under my breath. Soldiers had found me so quickly, and now that I'd killed one of my own, any order to bring me back alive would change. Strangely, I felt energized. Direct conflict made sense to me, and in this fight, I knew exactly what to do. Save Vilet and myself from a fate worse than death. All my training could do some good for once.

Beside me, she didn't glance my way, but I knew we were together in this. Our alliance was tenuous, but it held now. She offered me hope. I offered her protection. We'd see those through as far as we could go. We wouldn't die today.

Two more soldiers appeared, smeared with red body paint —Ares' battle signature. I didn't wear mine. Just a reminder that I didn't belong with their bloodthirsty group anymore. They towered, hulking but agile, in front of us. I knew both of them, but not well.

"Get behind me," I snapped, my palm following Vilet's shoulder without touching her, as if to place her there.

Blood already spattered my body from the first soldier. Fighting Queen Bellona's forces I was used to. Attacking Ares' soldiers, not so much.

It was a welcome change.

The rage I'd lately struggled against took hold, and I let it. Warriors of the Twin Armies were angry and violent and often unhinged. I knew the training these soldiers had endured. My body was ripped and broken and re-formed into rock, until I was a killing machine. Until I belonged. I craved that belonging so fiercely that it didn't matter that I belonged to this murderous group.

No more.

I saw blood, and blades, and darkness. Yells split the air.

I wasn't made a Sentinel for nothing.

The soldiers gurgled in their last breath before I stabbed downward twice, ending their torment.

Panting, half-wild, I turned back toward Vilet. Her hair hung around her face as she stared at my work in disbelief. She didn't look relieved. She looked like she was in shock.

I clenched my teeth. Vilet wasn't like me. She didn't choose violence, but it followed her anyway. Those men at the dock. Hell, even the way I'd grabbed her arm like a godsdamned simpleton, totally forgetting the trauma she'd just been through. And now...

A breeze blew against my skin, cooling my hands. They were drenched in blood. Was all that from the three I'd killed?

A shuffle.

Three more appeared right behind Vilet.

I saw red.

No.

Everything moved slowly. The soldier closest to her didn't have a weapon in his hand yet. As he reached for it, his fingers also groped forward toward Vilet. I knew what would happen.

Total annihilation—that was Ares' philosophy. I'd managed to keep my killing to soldiers, but I'd stood by idly too many times while innocent people suffered. This soldier would grab Vilet from behind, unsheathe his weapon, and slit her throat.

His fingertips brushed her skin.

Vilet startled. They'd appeared so quietly she hadn't noticed.

The fingertips became a caress, feeling their prey.

Not today, fucker.

I punched him over Vilet's shoulder to make him stumble back while I dispatched the two others. Fury guided my knife. I knew the moves. I knew the training. I knew everything they'd do before they did it.

Two down.

That left the one who'd dared to touch Vilet.

He held a knife now, but I didn't care. In a breathless, urgent struggle, both blades went flying. The soldier landed on his back with me on top of him. I actually smiled in his face as I held out my hand for my weapon.

Vilet obliged.

"You touch her," I snarled. "You die. In pain." After a few more breaths, I added, "Too bad there's not more time. I would have kept you alive for days."

He squirmed underneath me. Fear didn't change his expression, but it did light his eyes.

"This was the hand." I snatched it up, pinching the ends of his longest fingers. His eyes flew wide.

Ares' soldiers were taught not to scream, but it was hard not to when someone chopped off three of your fingers.

I stood and plunged the knife into his gut so far it pinned

him to the forest floor. It was sick how much enjoyment I got from that.

More running feet.

Shit. How many had the god of war sent?

Vilet gestured and flung herself over a rise. I followed.

And didn't see her. My heart careened against my ribs. She couldn't walk through the air like we could, right? No, I couldn't sense the residual magic.

Leaf litter shifted near my feet. She was under the leaves and dirt and pine needles. It lay thick enough here to hide her. And me. Was that what she meant by pointing me in this direction? But I didn't hide. I fought.

A spiraled second later, the truth hit me. I wasn't a fighter anymore. I'd die defending Vilet, but here, I didn't have to fight. I could hide with her until the immediate danger passed, no trail of bodies or magic to give us away. It wasn't the worst plan.

Pushing past the resistance in my limbs to stay still, I followed her lead, lying flat and covering myself with the deep litter on the forest floor. With my ear against the soil, I felt and heard the number of footsteps running our way. A company of soldiers, more than I could defeat on my best day. A second ago, I'd been hot-blooded enough to try. My attempt would have gotten us both killed.

Forcing calm back into my body so the leaves didn't rise with every breath, I counted running feet. They tramped over the hollow where I'd slaughtered our attackers, canvasing the area.

Vilet and I didn't move.

After what had to be almost an hour, the soldiers disappeared. Instead of instantly bursting from the leaf litter, I reached out in tiny movements, finding Vilet's hand. She responded, linking her fingers with mine. Relief, stronger than I would have suspected for such a small gesture, pierced me like a knife. I ran a thumb over the back of her hand.

She'd saved my life.

11

VILET

Nothing stirred.

Even Leander's hand, now holding mine as we lay under leaf litter, maintained the same warm pressure. His strong fingers felt sticky. That should have disgusted me, but it was like a constant heartbeat reminder that he had killed for me. Kept me safe. Chosen me over them.

One of the things clogging my throat with emotion was that he hid with me, too. The hardened soldier copied *my* choice to keep us alive. The combination made me hold Leander's hand harder.

Meeting Leander hadn't been a mistake. It would probably save me. I wanted to curl up in his lap and let him hold me, simply quiet for a while.

The forest itself was very quiet. No birds sang or rabbits rustled. Ares' soldiers had scared them away, but I hadn't heard them for what felt like a long time.

Finally, Leander moved. Exhaling, I rose too. Dirt fell off

us. I dashed it off my face and clothes as I scanned the trees, which were beginning to lighten with dark blue dawn.

"You look beautiful." Leander squeezed my hand.

His rich brown eyes took me in, but I seriously doubted I looked beautiful just then. My hair was ratty, with dead pine needles hanging off it. My dress was stained in a million ways and I had dirt on my face.

I waved him off, blushing and plucking something out of my hair.

He, by contrast, was the stuff of dreams. Men built like him should always be dirty and bloodstained, if their deep-set eyes showed compassion too. It hurt to look at him.

He pulled me to my feet. "That was a brilliant idea." He kept his voice low, in case more enemies waited to appear.

"It's what I have," I said, shrugging.

He drew closer. "Don't second-guess yourself. I saw a brave woman, a survivor, who also manages to be sexy as hell." The dimple appeared in his cheek.

If he hadn't already seen me have a panic attack and be imperfect in lots of ways, I'd think he was imagining a better version of me. But he wasn't. He knew about the panic and the ducks and the hatred I had for Ares. That was more than some friends back home truly understood about me. They knew my preference for sugar bread and how mud fish scared me and that summer was my least favorite season. Leander knew deeper things. He had witnessed parts of my trauma and shared my fragile hope for the future.

He had killed for me.

The corpses of Ares' soldiers bled into the inside of my eyelids with each blink, so I stared resolutely at Leander's face.

His warm confidence cooled. Questions flamed and died over his face. A hint of uncertainty showed he wasn't sure I was all right. I wasn't sure either. The bodies left in Leander's wake weren't innocent, but my thoughts spiraled around them like birds of prey, trying to make sense of what had happened.

Leander had killed, but he had killed for me. For us, to get away.

"I wasn't the hero here," I replied.

"Bullshit." But a tiny sparkle in his eye said he was pleased by my compliment. "But we do need to move. It's quiet now, but they'll send more."

My eyes fell on the spear symbol over his heart. *They,* not *we.*

I nodded, exhaustion seeping into my bones. We started walking. He took slower strides so I could keep up.

"You didn't... know any of those people, did you?" I asked. Our attackers were definitely from Ares' army, and most of them were demi-gods.

"I recognized them," he answered without emotion.

What kind of life could have made him this stoic in the face killing people? I tried not to think about the things he must have done on Eriset to earn his reputation, but the idea wormed its way into my cocoon of peace.

"We aren't allowed to make friends," he elaborated. "Just one of the reasons I liked talking to you. No one told me to shut up or stop, and you didn't know it was against the rules."

"I wasn't supposed to be talking to anyone either."

His brows lowered. "No?"

"It's safer not to."

He hummed his agreement. "I want to change that. I want us to talk to each other."

"About pasts too," I added, gauging his reaction.

His expression darkened. "That's fair. I want to know all of you. You should know all of me if you want, but I'm warning you, it isn't pretty." His gaze locked back on mine. "But I promise you on my blood and bone that I won't return to serving the Twin Armies. I'll die first."

A shiver ran down my back. His tone was steel. "You've saved me twice." I huffed a sardonic laugh. "I wish you didn't need to, but you did. That's enough proof for me."

A smile lit his face. Gods, he was gorgeous.

"Do you know how they found us so fast?" I asked.

The furrow in his forehead answered before his words could. "I've been thinking about that. They shouldn't have been able to appear right where we were."

"Is there"—I racked my brain—"some divine magic on you all the time?" I knew only the basics about demi-gods. All my experience was with humans.

"No. There might be a seer on the island, though. One of Cytherea's people..." he mused.

I chewed the inside of my lip. That didn't sound good. "Someone who can see where we are?"

He cut his gaze away. "Maybe."

"Then..." I didn't know how to finish the question. If someone could see where we were, no place was safe.

He met my eyes again. "This forest is ancient. There are bound to be places that have wards or barriers."

"Okay. Can you sense a ward?" I never could. The highest-ranking soldiers, if they were wealthy, could pay to have their armor warded, but it was a rare request and it took a long time, since Warders were in high demand.

"Sometimes."

I stepped over a fallen log. "So, we'll find a warded area and stay there until... Do you think the soldiers will stay longer to look for you? For us, I guess."

"One of the things that's kept the war going is how unpredictable he is. He might want to stay. I have a guess, but it's only that. I don't know as much as I wish I did."

I longed to reach out and take his hand. Whatever happened now, our fates went together. "My brother has a theory," I said, "that he never attacks on the first quarter moon."

Leander grinned, his frustration evaporating. "Any reason?"

I tipped my mouth. "Observation."

"What was it tonight?"

"Waning crescent."

"Out of luck, then."

We reached a boulder. Leander offered his hand to help me up. I took it. His firm grasp steadied my legs, which were getting shaky with fatigue. Once I scrambled to the top, he let go and climbed after me. I missed the warmth of his hand. It couldn't have been easy for him to admit how much he didn't know. For someone who'd kept a giant secret when we first met, he seemed completely honest now.

"So, you have a brother?"

I nodded. "Vash." His name was like a spell in its power. Honesty for honesty. It felt reckless to say aloud.

"Soldier?" he asked.

"Ropemaker. When I can, I want to get him out too." That godsdamned guilt came rushing back. How hard would it have been to stow him away on the ship too?

"We just need to find our island."

"Exactly."

The sky lightened to jewel blue. It was easier for us to see, but that meant it would be easier for anyone following us too.

I stumbled forward a few more steps, my breath coming in gusts. Leander didn't even act tired. *You can keep up. Come on. We're looking for wards.* But I had no idea how to find a ward or how close we might be.

Exhaustion came on strong. When it turned to shaking, I ground my teeth. This wasn't the time for my body to decide it was done.

Leander touched my elbow. "We can head back to the docks soon. Get a ship. Get the hell out of here and onto that island."

I gave him a shivery smile, but he clearly saw how my body had had enough. Add to that the hunger and shock and panic I'd just gone through, the triple orgasms and the lack of sleep. Of course I was done for. But Eriset women never gave up.

"Sounds good," I said, taking another step forward. My joints felt loose. I cursed under my breath.

"You're... wobbling." Leander sounded infinitely concerned, as if he'd never see any being wobble before. With his training, maybe he hadn't.

I let out a breathy laugh. "I'm fine. Let's go."

"May I carry you?"

He could easily have scooped me up, ground tilting, and gotten us out of there fast. Instead, he asked. And that sounded heavenly, although a part deep inside me with the ferocity of a badger hissed and spit at the idea. I told my pride to stand down and scrunched my lips in amused agreement.

This was ridiculous.

But I was right. It was heavenly.

12

VILET

Leander, so huge he was practically three of me, lifted me gingerly in his blood-stained arms. I held onto his neck, but I didn't need to. He cradled me securely against his chest. With each step, I rocked, and the images of the dead weren't only nightmares, but images to reassure me that the one who protected me was the best warrior here.

The next few miles were a blur. Leander never set me down, at least not until we reached shelter.

"Finally," he murmured, stepping into the cool dimness of a mountain cave. This one was a proper cave, not just a crevice like we'd hid in before. It had ceilings twice as high as Leander's head, with rough rock walls and a smooth floor.

As I swam up from my doze, I took a better look. The cave wasn't deep, more like a huge chunk dug out of the mountainside that offered a gorgeous view of the sky and tree-strewn hills.

Morning light bathed the planes of Leander's face as he

settled me on my feet. His touch on my shoulders was tender. "Steady?" he asked.

"Steady."

We looked in silence for a minute. Every breath I took tasted stony and fresh. I loved the air here—all pine and residual moonlight and carefree soil.

"I can tell there are wards here," he said. "I didn't even see this place until we were right outside it."

He must have been right, because the view was so clear, it was like we were on a stage. Only magic would have hidden this place.

"No one's coming for us. We can do this, Vilet." A shared flame of hope burned in his eyes, small but true.

The reality of this—running away with a stranger for the possibility of a new life—flooded my senses. I tensed as if I were standing at the edge of a tall cliff. Hope was tangible. And dangerous. And I wanted it so bad.

I tested my weight. My legs didn't shake anymore.

"Yes, we can," I said.

He nodded. That dimple again. We had survived a direct attack by members of the Twin Army. Maybe a peaceful future really was possible.

Something like embarrassment passed between us, as if we'd just professed our love, which we had in a way.

Emboldened, I cupped his cheek. His expression went molten.

Pressing me to him, he kissed me, long and soft and demanding. My stomach did flips. Every kiss with Leander was better than the last because I could give him more of myself and we knew more and more about what the other liked. How he managed to grind against me while kissing someone so much shorter, I didn't know, but I wanted him to keep going, keep rubbing that needy spot between my legs.

Finally, he let me go. A pang of disappointment was quickly replaced by practical things. "We should talk about when to get on the ship," I said when I could breathe again.

"Later." He still held me in his arms, eyes glazed from our kiss. Just one look at his swollen lips threatened to banish any other thought.

"It won't be easy, if we're sneaking on."

"Later." His warm lips and warm body touching mine silenced any more protests. He was gentle but insistent, just like he'd been in The Shell and Lemon.

Okay, no more planning.

His lips tasted mine, hot kisses trailing down to my neck. My breath grew short, all sensation bunching around his tongue at my throat and his long fingers at my hips, pressing me against the hard lump between his legs.

"Do you want me?" His words came out as humid air against the sensitive skin behind my ear. "I want you." It was a delicious question. Just checking, in case I had any more reservations. I didn't.

"Yes."

"How?"

"I want you to claim me however you like," I managed. My core was throbbing already, yearning for him to take.

"What if I like it rough?" His chest pressed to mine rose and fell raggedly, desperate, excited. The question was another honest piece of him peeled back. "What if I want to fuck you hard?"

"Do it."

"What if I want to stuff my cock down your throat before I drill you from behind?" His hot, gentle hands as they took off my clothes didn't match the violence of his words. He smoothed my cheek. I saw battle in his eyes—his desire to take care of me warring with the powerful soldier wanting to give commands.

"Two slaps," I rasped.

His grin was wicked. We got him out of his clothes. Those scars couldn't hide the beauty of that hard body. "Say I'm yours," he demanded.

I almost laughed. "You're mine."

He growled with pleasure. "Now get on your knees, my love. Show me you can take it."

His dick was thick with arousal when I knelt, my kneecaps grinding against the stone floor. Leander was already tall, but he looked monstrous from this angle—a formidable deathless male in all his glory. I caressed one of his muscular thighs before using it to ground myself. A lick to the tip and then I fed him in. I knew how he liked it—all the way in and down the throat—so I pushed forward.

"Ah!" he groaned, reaching down and gripping my hair. I bobbed until saliva started running down my chin. "That's a good girl."

The sunlight falling into the cave made it feel like we were on display, secluded and public at once. I sucked him with gusto, the feeling of being watched only adding to my arousal.

Once more, I pressed into him, fitting in the whole shaft. His muscles clenched under my hands, which he always kept free.

He drew me up to my feet again using my hair. Somehow, he did it without hurting me.

He controlled my body so fast I couldn't tell what motions he used to get me against the cave wall. My breasts and belly pressed flat against cold stone. Then his fingers were under me, between my legs, positioning me open for him. Open and sopping wet. His fingers didn't ask this time. They took. He found that spot I liked and rubbed ferociously. My whimper echoed in the cave.

"Yes," he murmured. "Take it. Take me." He pulled my hips so my back arched, presenting my ass to him. His cock replaced his fingers, driving in hard and deep.

I gasped.

"Yes," he said again, his stone-strong arm snaking around to circle my throat. He didn't squeeze, but held me against his body as he found a ruthless rhythm. His other hand fondled my breast, pinching the hard nipple. His arms were so much warmer than the stone wall. It was pleasure and it was pain. His sex was rough, but never so much I felt trapped. I could breathe. I could move. And, if I wanted to, I could slap him twice. Now, with his body slapping up into me, nothing could have made me do that. Caught in his arms, I craved every sensation—his hot panting in my ear, the wave of controlled muscles against my back, his blood-stained palms squeezing my breasts...

"Say I'm yours," I croaked.

He doubled the pace of his thrusts. I felt his relief, his passion, before he said a word. Breath heaving, he finally answered, "Mine. You're mine!"

Close now, he pinched me hard enough that I shouted, growing wetter.

"Come with me, Vilet," he commanded, the hand lowering to my clit where he gave relentless strokes.

I couldn't help but obey, gripping his arms so I didn't shudder to the floor. Our cries overlapped, echoing off the walls.

Sore and panting, I straightened and faced him, craning up to see his face. For all his ferocious lovemaking, his expression was soft. How lucky was I to have such a wild, caring lover? This must have been what peace felt like.

He hummed as he looked at me, deep and appreciative. "Mine," he said, voice low, trailing his finger softly down my shoulder to my breast.

"Mine," I repeated, laying my hand on his firm chest.

We smiled.

Getting a ship without Ares' army spotting us would be tomorrow's problem. Today, I was pretty sure I'd found love, something I never thought I'd find.

13

LEANDER

I woke with my arm around Vilet's waist. She was warm and soft as she breathed. I didn't deserve this, didn't deserve her.

The past day had been a whirlwind of lovemaking, broken only by gathering some food and water. I was insatiable for her, obsessed with giving her everything.

Now that it was the next morning the cave barely had enough light to see by. If we didn't move, the floor was warm enough, but the slightest shift was ice-cold. I held Vilet closer. She could have my heat.

This girl I'd just met had overcome so much, even in the past few days, all because of the war in Eriset that I helped fight. All my sharp edges kept scraping against her on accident.

The words echoed again. I didn't deserve her.

But I could protect her.

That would be a thousand times easier once we got off this godsdamned island. Ares was mad, but he was no fool. He loved a hunt, and I'd made myself the hunted. The best thing Vilet and I could do was leave. Now.

I nuzzled my face in her hair. She smelled like spice and lemons and something floral. The scent was as heady as a drink, so I filled my lungs with her again and again in slow, mindful inhales. Too bad we couldn't stay in this cave and hold each other longer, maybe repeat what we'd done yesterday.

I groaned with longing.

But with consciousness came a soldier's instincts, and those were all telling me I'd stayed too long already. Either Ares' army had left last night as planned or there was no telling how long they'd stay on Aphriso to look for me. Best to go now instead of sitting around any longer in uncertainty. Besides, I couldn't wait to start my new life with this incredible woman.

Vilet stirred. Maybe I'd woken her up with my noise.

"Vilet, my love." I carefully smoothed a lock of hair away from her cheek so I could see her more clearly. She stole my breath. Despite being held by an enemy soldier whose scars she must be able to feel down the length of her back, she looked more content than I'd ever seen her. I wanted to keep her safe and happy like this forever. "Wake up."

She sighed and snuggled closer.

Damn it. Why was this temptation harder to combat than an actual opponent? Being a hero to someone instead of a villain made me a better person, but made it a whole lot harder to disentangle the naked woman from my arms.

I tried again. "Vilet, we need to go." I splayed my fingers on her belly in one last attempt to cement this moment in my mind before I stood, leaving her to the chill.

While I dragged on my clothes, Vilet finally angled up. A tiny smirk crossed her lips as she looked at me.

I finished fastening my pants. "What?"

"Nothing."

I smirked back at her, offering a hand. She took it and stood. My skin sizzled as if I hadn't just held her in my arms all night.

Soon, we were both dressed. Worries weighed on Vilet again, just like they had on me once I was awake enough to remember them all. We didn't live in some painting where gods lived carefree in the forest somewhere. But we had each other, which was more than either of us ever expected to find.

Last night, we'd talked, half-delirious. Neither of us used the word *love,* but it was there like a shard of iron in my chest. Wrong. A liability. Worthy of punishment in Ares' army.

Well, fuck him.

It was hard to shake off years of mental habits. What I had with Vilet was strong enough to crack those habits, though, and begin to alter them into something else.

"Last push," I said. "Let's find that ship."

Hand in hand, we left safety of the cave wards.

"I saw three ships from Nalia at the docks when we were there," I explained quietly as we walked through the forest.

"Do you think they'll still be there?"

"If there were three, then there's a good chance at least one will still be docked when we arrive. We can request passage right before they leave."

"Or sneak on," she said.

"Not a Nalian ship," I countered. There were no better

sailors in the Eight Realms, and their ships were legendary. Better not to risk raising the alarm if we were found.

"Do you want to go to Nalia?" Vilet asked.

I shrugged. "There are lots of islands there. We could take one as our own." I scanned our surroundings before casting her a suggestive gaze.

She turned slightly pink. "Nalia's on the other side of the Eight Realms, right?"

I made a large open oval with my fingers. "Aphriso and Eriset are on this side"—I pointed to the upper left—"and Nalia's over here." I tapped the webbing of my hand at the lower right.

"Then that sounds perfect. And ships from Nalia go to Eriset sometimes, don't they?"

Her question surprised me. "Are you planning to visit?"

"No, but Vash is still there."

I grunted. *That's right.* She said he was a ropemaker, but if he was around Vilet's age, he'd get recruited to fight soon, more than likely. I didn't like his odds as a human in Ares' army. His chances might be slightly better in Bellona's military, but Ares' sister wasn't called the queen of bloodshed for nothing. Both of the Twin Armies were ruthless, and humans too often got caught in between.

Just the thought of Vilet back there trying to survive made me reach for her hand.

She blinked in surprise before tightening her grip on me.

Mine.

Our promise from last night.

We walked most of the way in silence. Her footfalls barely made a sound. There would be time to learn every facet of her once we got off Aphriso and landed somewhere Ares would never find us.

My ears piqued at every noise. Pinecones were footsteps. A breeze was a hissed breath. Once, from a distance, I thought I saw a skeletal horse, dark and pointed, clopping between the trees. It didn't act aggressive, so we let it be. Still, the closer we headed toward civilization, the more my body stiffened for combat.

Hope kept threatening to bubble in my chest that Ares' soldiers wouldn't return to attack me. Maybe they'd left. But that was the kind of thinking that got warriors killed. Even demi-gods.

I'd had friends—friends in passing, at least—who were demi-gods, and Ares burned five of them alive after trapping them in a building. Even now, the memory brought vomit to the back of my throat.

Muted voices meant Card was just through those trees. The scent of dust cut through the air. I set my jaw. For a moment I second-guessed myself. Was I really bringing Vilet back here?

But, I reminded myself, this was the closest port. Most of the others were clear across the island, over the mountains, and who knew what ships docked there? Card held our greatest chance for escape if we were willing to take the risk.

Worse case scenario was that Ares' forces were still there, looking for us. Unless they had that seer I suspected look right as we entered town, we could make it. Two people could slip through.

I crouched next to a large tree and peered through breaks in the branches to the city and sea beyond. Nalian ships, like

I'd seen before, bobbed on the waves. They were blackish-blue, almost iridescent, so they tricked the eye in open water. I'd always been a land-based fighter, or else Nalian ships might have scared the shit out of me.

Right now their famous speed and camouflage were a good thing.

Vilet, silent as a cloud, knelt next to me. I set a comforting hand on her knee.

Her stiffness told me she was nervous. I didn't blame her. I didn't have any demi-god powers besides the universal ones, but I'd been a warrior in the Eight Realms' most dangerous country for decades. I could sense fear. It didn't drown Vilet, but it prickled her skin and shallowed her breath. In a fight, it would make her movements more desperate and less precise.

I glanced at her and she met my eye. She wouldn't have to fight, not with me around. She had a protector now. I offered my best carefree smirk, as if all we had to face were those bastards who'd attacked her behind that building.

Almost as one, we moved swiftly, keeping to the shadows. This method of skittering from one spot to the next grated on me. It was so slow. But if I walked through the air with Vilet in tow, the residual magic would leave a trail Ares' soldiers could easily follow. I could track as well as any beast, so I knew others could too.

Quiet. Quick. We broke through the tree line into the light. No sign of soldiers from Eriset, besides the little give-aways we always left behind—signs over pub doors declaring a shortage of wine, a slight smear of red paint on the corner of a building... We slunk close to outbuildings and shadowy corners, making our way toward the sea. I searched every corner as we passed, listening for voices, sensing divine magic. No obvious threat presented itself, but still grew more and more uneasy.

Eventually, we made it close enough to see the nearest Nalian ship bobbing ahead of us. I scanned for weaponry—none visible. This was a cargo or passenger ship. My guess was cargo. This section of the port seemed geared for business, with only a few wary, bustling people attending to their crates. The only other time I'd traveled to Aphriso with the army, I'd seen a nicer area down the coastline where people could board luxury vessels undisturbed by the rabble at the main port.

I raised a brow at the big craft, and Vilet nodded. That would do.

Again, I scanned for others dressed like me. No soldiers out on patrol. This was Cytherea's Realm, but Ares liked to flex his power as much as possible in other gods' domains, when he was there. The lack of a military presence suggested he really had left.

Last time I was here, I hadn't been promoted, so I prowled the streets of Card, keeping people in line. I cringed at the memory. Like with Vilet's attackers, I enjoyed putting people in their place. If something seemed off, my training said to act fast, not ask questions. Vilet, on the other hand, might have talked if she were in that situation, like she did with me, not assuming I was a monster even after I killed multiple men in front of her.

Emotion toward Vilet surged up in me. I didn't know what emotion, exactly. The others and I never talked about how we felt about things. But this feeling was strong, as if I were glowing and on fire at the same time—good and painful.

I took her hand again.

If they're not patrolling and they haven't left, where are they? The nagging question wouldn't let go, despite all evidence telling me not to worry.

Then, a horrifying thought. Were they not on the streets because they were all looking for me?

Despite my battle upbringing, despite everything I'd seen, my blood chilled at the idea. After my level of treason, killing me would be a last resort. Ares, and even soldiers I'd fought beside, would gladly pluck me apart piece by bloody piece, keeping me alive until the last second.

Vilet squeezed my hand. "This'll be good," she said softly, indicating the ship.

The blue-black ship loomed above us. Its hull was almost scaly, as if the boat itself were some creature.

A creature that would take us far away from here.

I blew out a breath. "Should be."

Against a nearby post, a sailor leaned carelessly, paring her nails with a knife. She was slim and dark-skinned, at least compared to the light skin people from Eriset had. Her clothes had so many layers and sashes and little bags that she probably hid more weapons in there somewhere. I would if I were her, here alone. But she didn't strike me as somebody to be concerned about. She was more like a shark who wouldn't bother with anything not bleeding.

We approached. "Is this your ship?" I asked.

She barked a laugh and looked up from her dirty finger-nails. Her expression changed when she saw us. She scanned us both so completely it was obvious she enjoyed what she saw.

Vilet frowned. "Do you work on this ship?" she revised.

The sailor tossed the paring knife in the air and caught it expertly before tucking it away. "Second mate."

"Where's the captain?" I asked.

"Gods know where." She sighed. "He likes to find a good time whenever we land, if you know what I mean." Her eye twitched, but it could have been a wink.

"When are you heading back to Nalia?" I asked.

"Depends." She straightened, but it was like a cat when it stands straighter, tail in the air, daring you to come closer.

"We can pay you whatever you want," Vilet said quickly.

I kept my face neutral. We didn't have much money, but we could get more if that was what it took to get out of here.

The sailor's eyebrows rose, making her piercing bisecting one of them glint in the light. "We're happy to hear that. Curious too." Her excitement morphed into suspicion. She inspected us again, this time with a more critical eye. Smacking her lips, she declared, "Get aboard. Quick. Wouldn't want Ares to know you're here."

Ice shot through my body, but it was the most logical assumption. King Ares didn't often visit Aphriso. Maybe our skin or our voices somehow gave us away. Brave to allow us on board her ship, then.

I gave her a curt nod and backed toward the gangplank.

The sailor made some motions at the crew to stay quiet about us. A couple of them had been watching us from over the rail as they prepared the ship for its next voyage. Both were dark-skinned, like the woman we talked to, with a variety of piercings and mismatched clothing. They looked like they'd come from a hurricane that mixed all Eight Realms together.

I touched the small of Vilet's back to guide her up the

gangplank to the deck, while glaring at the sailors on board. If any one of them so much as touched her, they'd have to be scraped off the planking. None of them looked inclined to come close, since I was there. I knew the effect I had on others. Years with Ares' army had taught me how to intimidate with my height, my face, my physique, and my weapons. Everything I had and was.

Vilet looked back at me. I toned down my expression, my stomach twisting that she'd seen that look. That deathly stare belonged to my life with Ares, not my new life with Vilet.

Her lips pursed as if she were holding in a smile. Okay, maybe she didn't mind that I'd threaten on her behalf. *I swear, this woman...*

We moved out of sight of the dock, but no one led us to any room.

Vilet drew close, her body half-flush against mine, to whisper. I bent to listen. "She didn't say a number."

I grunted in response. It was true. More negotiations should have come first.

The ship creaked and rolled underneath us. It was a fairly large vessel, not as large as some of the warships I'd seen, but bigger than many of the cargo vessels in the port.

"We'll negotiate on the way," I whispered back. Being this close to Vilet again, practically hearing an analysis of our situation whirr in her brain, made me hungry and hard for her. I'd never get anything done with her around.

"We should figure out when they're setting off," she replied. Her voice was steady but her neck flushed.

"Soon. Otherwise I'll pull the captain off his mount myself."

Vilet's eyes glazed. I knew that look by now. But it wasn't the time.

"We'll be sailing to Nalia to find our island before you know it," I promised. A longing filled me to arrive there, free from threats, where all we had to do was survive and hold each other.

When did I become such a romantic? I gave Vilet a crooked smile, and she smiled back. Well, I wanted to do un-romantic things to her too, like rip her clothes down the middle to fondle her breasts, like making her chest heave and hair drip with sweat as she sobbed with pleasure.

We were so close to freedom. We had different reasons to run, but we wanted exactly the same kind of freedom at the end.

Peace.

Gazing into Vilet's eyes, watching the heartbeat in her neck in my peripheral, I hoped peace was real. We weren't out of danger yet, but we were closer than I'd ever been before, and I'd let nothing take this hope from me.

14

VILET

"I'm going to help them load the supplies. Might get us out of here faster," Leander said.

I released his waist. Holding onto him made me feel anchored. This plan to escape to Nalia was crazy, wasn't it? But with him, it felt possible, a dream so beautiful I ached.

"All right."

I'd seen the look he sliced toward every sailor aboard when we stepped on the ship. Even if the safety it gave only lasted an hour, it definitely had an effect. No one shied away, but they gave us plenty of room.

Not long now. I sent the thought to Vash. Where was he now? If soldiers knew I was on the run, had they interrogated him. Was he safe? Was he even alive?

Of course he was. I had to believe it, or else my impending happy ending would have been the worst kind of selfishness. Besides, I'd find a way for him to join us eventually. Yasmin still had parents, so I wasn't sure about her.

So many unknowns, and we still hadn't left the dock.

I wrapped my arms around myself as I watched Leander descend the gangplank. For such a huge person, he stepped almost silently. A threat to the potential threats around us. That bigness that could have scared me was a comfort now. I exhaled against the salty air.

A scream split the air. My gut turned to water. *What...?*

I froze. A second cry joined the first. Footsteps scuffled over boards. A fight. Something was wrong.

My legs weighed as much as twin boulders, but I swept up the end of a rope that had a metal clasp on it that was lying near my feet. Metal wasn't the best, if *he* was here, but I couldn't see anything else that could count as a weapon.

The sailors on board rushed to the gangplank where Leander had disappeared moments before. Steel rasped against sheaths and pounded against hard objects. Shouts and curses escalated the chaotic racket until there was no doubt of what was happening.

Ares' soldiers had found us.

Gripping the thick, metal-tipped rope, I forced myself toward the railing. Leander was in trouble, and it sounded like he needed help. First, I would look through the slats, not above, to choose the right thing to do.

Was there anything I could do to prevent the inevitable now? Even Leander wouldn't be a match for a whole group of Ares' soldiers at once, could he?

Boots stomped on the planking and the sailor woman appeared. "Raise anchor!" she cried. The sails whipped and bellowed above her as if to respond. Others on board bustled around, performing nautical tasks I couldn't guess at, since I'd spent the short voyage from Eriset to Aphriso hidden below deck.

I knelt on the hard wooden boards, tarred smooth, and peered between the slats. At first, I couldn't see Leander, because everyone dressed in some variation of Leander's molded armor. No Ares. He would have stood out even in that crowd. The king had only sent his cronies. All of them, by the look of it.

Then, there he was! Fighting, defending the gangplank, trying to stop anyone from getting up. A man shrieked as he fell halfway off the dock and was crushed as the ship rocked up on a wave. I winced at the scrape of the heavy hull against the mooring. Leander left two more corpses in his wake, but the rest of the soldiers had obviously gotten the same training.

My heart thundered in my chest, narrowing my vision. If the ship pulled away, I might survive, but Leander wouldn't. I shot a glance over my shoulder at the woman shouting orders —"All hands! All hands!"

Survival tugged at me.

But then, what would I have to live for? If I couldn't believe in the dream of freedom, of love, what was the point?

A bone cracked in the fight below. Leander doubled over. Was it his bone? Four soldiers were instantly on him. Four was too many. They'd kill him.

"Leander!" I screamed before I could stop myself.

He looked at me, but so did all the soldiers. Two of them peeled off and muscled their way past Leander up the gangplank.

I spread my feet, squeezed the rope in my fist, and spun it

in a circle as fast as it would go. The heavy metal end just missed me more than once.

Nalian sailors met the soldiers at the top of the gangplank, but not enough to ward them off. The rest of the crew were so busy raising anchor and whatever else ships needed to sail away that they couldn't respond in time to help me.

With a shriek, I flung the rope at the first soldier's eye. The soldier cursed, his hands flying to cover the bleeding wound. I hit my mark, but the rope lost all its momentum.

I didn't have time to try the same thing again with the other one. And another. And another. More warriors just kept running onto the deck.

I ran, dropping the rope. There were doors in the raised sections of the deck, but I knew better than to go below. I'd trap myself. Where, then? Where?

The deck didn't offer much shelter. I sprinted up the stairs leading to the ship's wheel. From here, maybe I could jump off, or buy time...

I didn't have a plan. This wasn't my home. I didn't know all the hiding places, but I had to survive.

Sounds of fighting continued below on the dock. Was Leander all right? A new, surprised voice joined them. Other sailors? The absent captain? Surprise meant they were probably not with Ares. Better than the alternative, but not good enough to get us out of this.

I scanned the lofted area for a new weapon. Everything looked dark and smooth as the planking on the deck. I cursed, tears edging my vision.

A soldier topped the right-hand stairs while another topped the left-hand stairs. I was surrounded.

"Vilet!" Leander's shout broke through the air. His feet weren't quiet this time, barreling across the deck. He ran recklessly, not quite himself, with that slash across his middle. Not deep, it looked like, but bloody.

I saw him run, streaked with blood, saw the soldiers approach me, and knew, in a moment of calm, that he wouldn't reach me in time.

Time stretched wildly, like candy. Any second it would break.

A sword flashed from the left-hand soldier. He didn't threaten. Real monsters didn't offer an explanation or a chance to escape.

Had I tried hard enough? My brother's sweet words returned to my mind. Yes, I hadn't given up. I'd been strong. I'd escaped and fought and believed in hope. I'd fallen in love.

Maybe Leander would find his beach. He'd survive this heartbreak. He was a warrior, after all.

A tear rolled down my cheek as I saw him move, desperate, each step taking too long. We locked eyes.

"I love you." With all the chaos around us, I didn't know if he heard me. But he'd understand anyway.

I only got partway through my confession before Ares' soldier stabbed me through the heart.

15

LEANDER

"NO!" I shrieked, sounding like some feral animal as the soldier stabbed Vilet. Blood gushed from the wound as she slumped. It wasn't a torturing slice to the stomach; it was an instant kill through the heart. The angle of the deck stopped my view of his second strike— to the neck, I knew.

The heart. The neck.

I couldn't see through my pain and rage. I had no thought.

As I reached the platform with the ship's helm, two of Ares' soldiers waited for me, standing like demons above Vilet's body.

Something violent happened, because I came to in the middle of smashing one soldier's face unrecognizable. My hands dripped with gore. Both soldiers, demi-gods by the look of it, slumped like bleeding puppets. I couldn't tell which was which, their faces were so mashed.

Heaving in breath, I turned to Vilet, sprawled between them. A furious sob ripped from my throat as I dragged her onto my lap. Her eyes were open, and she had deep wounds in her chest and neck.

She was dead.

The gangplank scraped as the Nalian sailors managed to haul it back in. Free of its anchor, the ship lurched, heading out to sea.

Hopefully, for the remaining crew's sake, I'd taken care of all of Ares' soldiers who had attacked us. My mind sputtered in chaos. I remembered killing some on the dock, getting the ones on the ship. Ares wasn't among them... as if I could have killed him anyway. He could still travel through the air right in front of us any second. That, or melt the rivets in the ship's hull and send us to the depths.

I'd welcome the fight. I might even welcome death.

I rocked Vilet's body. *I was supposed to protect you.* This was all my fault. The killing blow hadn't technically come from me, but I wasn't fast enough to save her. She'd counted on me, and I failed.

It didn't matter that the ship was pulling away to Nalia. I didn't want my island anymore, not without her on it.

I doubled over, ready to be sick as I cradled her in my arms. My existence was tied to hers. What could we do now?

My mind spiraled over itself, not comprehending. Death had never felt like this before. I'd seen plenty of it, and it was a shame or a travesty or a loss. This was lightning killing me from the inside. This was reality ripping itself inside out.

She trusted me. I thought she *could* trust me. To her, I was a hero, or at least a protector—someone capable of using my evil training for good. That should have been enough to save her. I was a warrior, a powerful demi-god, and I loved her.

I loved her.

Gods, the way she looked at me as she used her last breath to tell me she still loved me, even though I couldn't reach her...

I should have saved her. I was a demi-god, and she was a human.

She's a human. She's a human who has died.

Something ticked in my brain. Humans could have an afterlife.

I straightened, scrubbing the snot and tears from my face. It only took two coins, and Hades would accept dead humans into the Far Realm. The one place Ares refused to go.

Gathering Vilet in my arms, I stood. At the bottom of the stairs was, I assumed, the captain, ready to take the helm. He was young, like his mate, the woman. Greenish scales glinted in his skin when they caught the sunlight.

"Take us to the Far Realm," I barked.

He made a doubtful face.

I cut off my initial response, summoning all the threat I could muster. My promotion to Ares' guard wasn't for nothing. "I don't care what it takes to get there. This is not a request. Take us to the Far Realm now!"

16

VILET

L eander holds me.

No, not me.

I can see him from above. It's my body.

Tears gush down his face. Blood smears us both, but he didn't hurt me. Ares' soldiers did. It feels like that happened a long time ago. Even the scene below me of the ship and the sailors and Leander shouting orders as he cradles me looks misty. It's sad like a storybook is sad, but I'm compelled to watch.

The captain mans the helm and the dark Nalian ship changes course. I stay with Leander, hovering above him.

Time slips.

Day turns to night.

Leander smoothes my hair and pulls two coins from his pocket. Two coins. Are we going to the Far Realm?

Something in me recognizes this idea: body, coins, Far Realm.

Am I dead?

I feel like I'm slipping with the time. I think another day passes. I *want to speak to Leander, but I have no voice. I only have watchfulness, but it's like watching through water. Everything blurs out of focus. Even Leander's drawn face as he strains to see the horizon.*

The ship passes the gap in the Bridge. I remember that geography. Now we're in the Stygian Sea. No one but the dead go on the Stygian Sea.

But I guess I'm the dead.

Time slips, water slips, I slip further away.

Waves grow black, outlined in angry white, bucking the ship like a wild animal. It tips and rocks with the mountainous waves, down in a trough, up on a peak, splashed and shaken.

The storm passes. Clouds fuzz out sunlight.

In a moment of clear sight, I can see the ship like an arrowhead slicing through the water while, underneath it, encompassing it, a creature swims in the same direction. If it surfaces, they'll sink. Its slowly waving tail, as thick as the main deck, passes them as it swims by.

Leander spends most of his time in the front of the ship, looking out, sometimes talking to me. I understand why he doesn't want to stay with the body. I loved it, but it's used up now.

His face is sad, with deep furrows. He paces sometimes. The blood is gone and a bandage wraps his stomach.

He talks to me but I can't talk back.

Another storm attacks.

Leander and the sailors are wet and exhausted. The sailors are angry at Leander, who remains immovable as stone.

The ship grows hazier. I float near the crow's nest, but Leander still sees land before I do.

He's excited, energized. He's not pacing slowly anymore, but quickly. He goes to the body and talks to it.

The weather turns black again. Angry clouds coat the sky. Rain lashes through me to the deck.

As we draw close to the dark beach, with beings bustling around like the sailors do, tiny in the distance but growing larger, my sight becomes clearer.

Everything has color—blues and greens and the red around Leander's eyes. The purple of the clouds.

And I can think. I can want.

I want to let Leander know I'm here. I want to talk to him. I want to see my family again.

I don't want to disappear.

Feelings return too. I didn't realize they were gone.

I hurt.

I love.

Shouting on the beach as we draw close. The workers there seem surprised to see a ship. There's no port, only a jetty.

Leander picks up my body, an ugly sight now, and treats it carefully, lovingly, as if I were alive. Holding me carefully, he jumps off the side of the ship and swims, then wades, the distance to the shore.

I love him for it. I love him for everything. I want to be with him and tell him it will be okay, that he can still be happy.

My eyes sting. I'm crying.

"Here are the two coins!" he shouts, waving them in the air. "Where do I put her? How does she come back to life?"

Beach workers, demi-gods with frightening shapes, surround him, taking the coins and showing him where to go.

I follow Leander as he runs up the beach with me in his arms.

A current runs through me. It tugs me toward the ground.

Toward him.

I see a pale woman with black lips and antlers standing gracefully where the sand meets pine forest. When Leander gets close to that spot, my whole body jerks as if I've been flung, and my sight goes black.

Sand is cold underneath me. The black is the back of my eyelids.

17

VILET

I opened my eyes.

Leander choked, rain dripping off his face like tears as he looked down at me. Agony pierced the relief in his expression, deepening his dimple. His clothes and hair clung to him.

I was lying on wet sand. Cold wind whipped around us, and the surf sounded loud, as if my ears had been stuffed before. I shivered.

Leander released a sob and bent over to hold me more closely. His warm body blocked the downpour. "I'm sorry," he murmured into my neck before drawing a thumb carefully over the front of my throat.

Memories of the past few days felt like dreams. They clicked into place now, realizations hitting me a fiercely as the rain. Ares' soldier had stabbed me there.

I gasped and bucked.

Leander let go immediately.

I'd been stabbed in the heart too. My hand flew to the

spot. My clothes had no tear, and the skin underneath was clammy but intact. I didn't recognize the fabric.

Leander's long fingers moved to join mine as I explored the place where I should have had a wound, but he pulled back. I looked at my own fingers. Nothing, not even dried blood. I turned my gaze to Leander again.

"Am I...?" I had no idea how to phrase the question. My whole being was a question.

"Welcome to the afterlife." The low voice was female.

Leander adjusted into a defensive stance. Standing above us was the tall goddess with white skin, black lips, and antlers. Like a nightmare come to life, she looked like a ghost.

I tensed. I'd never seen a being like this. Her power dwarfed mine, and even seemed to overpower Leander.

The apparition's gaze slid from me to Leander and hardened. "It can be disorienting to arrive here. Help her to her feet."

"This is the afterlife?" I croaked. Despite the torrent of water around us, my throat was dusty-dry. She had welcomed me, after all. That probably meant she wouldn't eat me or something.

If this was the afterlife, did that mean that the friends I'd lost on Eriset would be here too? Did that mean I couldn't return to see my brother?

Leander gently stood me up. Partly because I felt weak and partly because I didn't want him to leave my side, I wrapped my arm around his waist and held on.

"It is," said the ghostly woman. "This isn't the best part of it. But congratulations, you've arrived." Her smile was thin.

Something was off. Those red eyes didn't echo the smile on her lips. I gripped Leander and his solid core of muscle closer.

"What is your name, human?" she asked.

"Vilet."

"We have a place for you out of the rain."

Out of nowhere, my throat constricted. Those words plucked a string buried deep in my heart. A place for me. Out of the rain.

"Thank you for your heroic service," the goddess added tightly, shifting to Leander.

Leander scoffed gently through his nose, as if she were mocking him. Did he not believe he had saved me?

But the more urgent issue was the ghostly woman's tone. Dismissive. She wanted Leander to leave.

"He was heroic to bring me here," I said. More memories crowded in, of storms, of pacing endlessly on the deck, of washing my body and changing the filthy clothes. I looked down. In the rainy gloom, it was hard to make out every detail, but the burgundy dress was beautiful. Not fancy or frilly, but crisscrossed with iridescent strips and soft against my skin. It had long sleeves and a neckline that showed my collarbone.

I squeezed Leander's waist. I could feel the bandage underneath his clothes, which hadn't changed. "I want to stay with him."

Leander didn't meet my eyes. Instead, he stared at the ghostly woman. "What is this place like that you've prepared for her?"

"Queen Persephone has created a new underworld for the humans." A glint of pride or joy lit up her black eyes. It made her look alien. "It is vast and you can find your own place in it.

There are rolling green hills and cozy cottages, rivers and lakes."

At that, Leander did finally look at me, but the look was quick and regretful.

My skin prickled, but, strangely, my heartbeat didn't kick up. I hadn't noticed because of the shock and the cold before, but I had no heartbeat. My anxiety pitched higher. "I want Leander to stay with me. If... he wants to stay." The sudden idea that he might not want to spend the rest of his immortal life in the Far Realm, famous for its mystery and darkness, hit me like a punch.

I loosened my grip a little, to give him permission to make his own choice. Hopefully, he would stay.

"This demi-god cannot stay with you," the antlered woman cut in. "There are plenty of humans there, and we do not have the resources to take in every person who wants to stay with the human spirits. Even if it is unusual for humans to be hand-delivered."

"Vilet." Leander's chocolatey voice was meant only for me. He gazed down at me beside him, rain streaming down both our faces. "I let you die. You don't have to stay with me." He set his jaw hard enough to cut.

I furrowed my forehead. "You didn't let me die. It wasn't your fault. You saved me. I love you, Leander."

"But I couldn't protect you." His throat moved in a hard swallow. The agony in his gaze made it hard to look at him.

"You tried. You made me feel safe. Even right now, I feel safe because you're here. You can't control everything."

"They were coming after *me*," he bit out. Bitterness coated the words. Drops that weren't rain joined the rest of the water on his cheeks.

"I don't regret a single second we spent together." To prove it, I rose up on my tiptoes.

After a second, he responded and bent down to meet my kiss.

"Mine," I whispered warm against his lips.

Remembering the goddess, I lowered myself again and faced her. "My lady," I began, unsure of who she was, "either both of us go, or neither of us do."

"Human spirits cannot leave the Far Realm," she answered. "Their existence is tethered here. I assure you, the underworld is beautiful. We can fetch you anything you want. There is beauty and rest forever."

Not without Leander. "Who can I ask to allow him to stay?"

Leander cast me a complicated look woven with hope and doubt.

"Lord Hades or Lady Persephone."

King Hades himself? I should have expected that answer, but it rattled me to the bone. The god of the dead was legendary, terrifying. And who was Lady Persephone? I'd heard no legends of another ruler in the Far Realm.

Steeling myself, I said, "Then let me talk to them."

❧ 18 ❧

VILET

The goddess disappeared. I shot a look up at Leander.

"Hold on, and hold your breath," he said solemnly. His drawn face and cut jaw didn't betray any excitement about what we were about to do. Would he rather leave and find his beach instead of staying with someone that reminded him of failure? I should have asked him outright. Now I was taking us both to talk to King Hades himself.

I obeyed, and a second later everything went black. Black as if no colors had ever existed, as if I were being squeezed in the space between space and would never get out...

My feet touched hard ground again. Leander rubbed my upper back soothingly while I caught my breath.

Just ahead of us, as if waiting, the antlered goddess pushed open a door to let us into Hades' palace.

It had to be Hades' palace. This castle was the grander than anything I'd ever imagined. It was black and pointed as an ice shard. Beautiful and nightmare-ish inside. I squeezed Leander's rough hand as if to say, *Look at this!*

We were walking through the stories of my childhood, rich and magical in a way my ordinary life never was.

But I didn't have time to fully take in the surreal experience of walking through *Hades' palace* because the antlered goddess led me and Leander too quickly.

Two large beings with bear-like faces stood on either side of a large black door. They opened the door when they saw the ghostly woman approaching. My stomach tightened. This was so far outside anything familiar. If I hadn't died already, I'd expect to here, simply from the danger and strangeness in every corner. At least I had Leander with me in this castle of lovely horrors.

The door opened into a long room, stretching right and left. It smelled of wine. Multiple naked women—definitely deathless, since they were unnaturally tall and muscular, with feathered wings and bird-like features—stood guard opposite where we entered. A trough ran parallel to our wall with a stream running through it. The goddess confidently strode (or floated) ahead over a black stone bridge before turning left to the thrones.

The thrones.

Where Hades and—what had the goddess said?—Persephone stood. They talked close together, standing between one black throne studded with black roses and skulls, and another made of delicate intertwining branches coated with black and green moss. When they turned to look at us, Hades' gaze sliced across us like a blade. He wore an expensive-looking black suit and a dusting of dark beard across his pale skin. Lady Persephone, shorter than he was, wore a long purple dress with pink flowers embroidered into the bottom of the skirt. She had lovely dark hair and earnest blue eyes that complemented her light brown skin. They couldn't have looked more opposite or more beautiful. Awe and fear actually hurt, the feelings were so strong.

"Marzanna," Hades said sharply. He hadn't expected us. "We've finished holding court."

Beneath my arm, I felt Leander's breath grow quick and shallow. He'd never faced the god of the dead either. The only one Ares feared.

"Lord Hades," the goddess answered smoothly, "Vilet has just arrived at the docks." She extended one hand to the side without looking back. "She is a human spirit."

"Intact," Hades commented, with a look to Persephone, whose lips quirked into a half-smile.

Marzanna continued. "She wants this male to stay with her in the underworld. He is a living demi-god. Correct?" She turned to head for Leander's acknowledgment.

"I am. And I do want to stay with Vilet. I'll do anything you ask."

My tense shoulders relaxed. I couldn't help a smile from creeping over my face.

Hades settled into the rose and skull throne, which I'd already guessed was his. He caressed an eye socket in the armrest with one finger. "The underworld is for humans." In his deep, cultured voice, the declaration sounded absolute.

I released Leander and stepped forward, knees shaking. I'd already died. What could Hades do to me that was worse than that? I didn't let myself consider the options before I bowed low to the ground. "Lord Hades, god of the dead, please hear—"

"And Queen Persephone," Hades commanded.

"And Queen Persephone. Please hear my request. My only wish is for Leander to have permission to stay with me here."

"Why? Many spirits arrive alone, but they aren't alone forever."

I hated the implication of his words. As much as I longed to see Vash again, I didn't want him coming here any time soon.

"Hades!" I didn't look up, but the new voice had to be Persephone's. Then, to me, "Why do you want him to stay?"

"I love him."

A short silence. Persephone again. "It's not unheard of for a human and a demi-god to fall in love." I had the feeling she wasn't talking to me anymore.

"It's not unusual for them to fuck," answered Hades.

Persephone sighed, maybe exasperated. "If they're really in love, I think we should let him stay."

I chanced a look at the powerful couple. Hades stared at his queen with something intense and mischievous in his eyes. They were having a conversation I couldn't understand.

"I made the underworld," Persephone said suddenly, like she was playing a game and just earned a point.

Hades raked a hand through his hair. Turning back to us, he said, "Don't make it a habit of bringing these people to me, Marzanna. You know what happens with precedent. But Persephone wants to make an exception. Yes, he can stay."

I leapt to my feet and wavered, forgetting how weak I was. Leander was by my side instantly. I beamed at him.

"Oh!" I turned back to Hades and Persephone. "Can I... Could I ask for one more thing?"

Leander's protective arms flexed around my back where he held me steady.

"I have a brother, in Eriset. He doesn't know what happened to me. I want him to know I'm okay."

When Persephone's big eyes softened, I grew hopeful.

"She asked us directly," Persephone said to Hades.

Hades pursed his lips. "So do many others. We can't do everything."

"We can do something."

"Let him bring the message." He gestured in one brutal, elegant motion toward Leander.

"Yes," Leander said swiftly.

I opened my mouth to protest.

"Yes, Lord Hades and Queen Persephone, I'll take the message to Eriset, and then I'll return." Leander faced me. "I can do this for you. Let me do this for you."

He looked so excited, so sincere, that I couldn't say no. It would have been cruel. Leander didn't have to prove anything to me—I knew he loved me and would have given up his own life to protect me if he could—but he needed this chance to forgive himself. It was all but written on his forehead.

"It's settled," Hades declared.

Persephone hunched her shoulders in child-like excitement. "You'll love the underworld, Vilet! And if you can think of any way to make it better, please let me know." She couldn't have been more different from the menacing god of the dead who sat next to her.

"Thank you, Queen Persephone!" I said, bowing again. "And King Hades."

Leander echoed my gesture as Marzanna ushered us back out of the throne room. We linked hands again while we made our way out of the palace. The underworld Persephone talked about obviously wasn't in there.

I couldn't stop blinking. Hades and Persephone. The whole interaction left me dazed.

But the crux of it was that Leander could stay, but not before he found my brother and delivered my message.

"We're from the Kastanea province," I explained once we were outside. The rain had let up somewhat. "Don't tell him everything. Just tell him I'm all right, but I can't see him. Because I *will* be okay now. You know, as soon as you come back."

New life lit up Leander's face since he'd gotten his assignment. Nervousness twisted my insides since demi-gods didn't have the same chance at an afterlife. But Leander was tough. He'd find his way back to me.

"I'll tell him," he said, stroking my wet cheek with his thumb. "Find us a good place near the water."

"With ducks?"

"Obviously."

We smiled at each other, bittersweet promise shining in our eyes, as Leander left and I let Marzanna lead me away to a place where I could finally find peace.

EPILOGUE: VILET

I dipped my toes in the cool water. Tiny waves lapped up on shore from the moving, flower-scented air. I inhaled a deep breath, glad I could still enjoy that luxury even though my heart had stopped.

Apart from being surrounded by actual spirits, I didn't feel dead. In fact, I felt more alive here than I had on Eriset or Aphriso. My chest slowly, slowly unclenched, and I was able to take big belly breaths whenever I thought about how Ares would never set foot in the Far Realm. When I met him, Lord Hades had been sharp, regal in a way I wasn't used to, but he didn't strike the same kind of unpredictable terror in me that Ares did. Hades had reasons for the things he did. He didn't strike out at innocents. He didn't adore blood. And yet Ares feared this place more than any other.

This place where I could rest.

I splashed my bare foot again into the wave. The pebbles underneath massaged the sole.

The underworld was actually underground, but it didn't

feel like it most of the time. The stone ceiling was so high I forgot it was there sometimes. The land was as vast as a province. I'd found this spot next to a lake that had an island on it. I'd always wanted to explore something like that as a kid. Plus, others from Eriset stayed nearby. We didn't talk about what happened to us, but we didn't have to. My new neighbors were kind, and understood me in a way that people from the pastoral Realm of Kantharos or another peaceful Realm couldn't. I was still meeting new people when I had the energy, but here, there was no rush. I'd find friends and relatives in time, and we could all eat together and not be afraid.

The only thing missing was Leander. Time moved differently here, so I couldn't be sure how long he'd been gone, but it felt like a couple weeks. The little house I'd picked out (Marzanna had said I could have it without any trade or formality or fuss) was ready for him.

Funny to think that we had known each other for less time than we'd now been apart. But sometimes you just knew.

I should have been afraid of Leander, but I never was. Not for a moment. At least, not after he explained himself after escaping from Ares. Even when I knew the smart thing was to be afraid, he'd give me a sultry look that managed to convey compassion and admiration too. He showed me the power I'd had all along that hadn't been able to flourish.

I missed him. That first day, he'd asked me what I wanted him to do to me. Now, I had plenty of ideas.

I scanned the hills that rolled away from the lake's edge. Gnarled trees, beautiful in their strangeness, loaded with lanterns, dotted the landscape. And beyond, there was—

That figure walking this way. Was that...?

I jumped to my feet. Good food and drink had returned my strength.

The figure was tall and sure and handsome as hell. I started running.

Leander paused, grinning. He opened his arms to let me leap into them. "Vilet!"

I collided with his chest. "Leander!" The last bit of tension in my body started to melt.

He held me up and cradled my head, pressing his lips to mine. He smelled like desert and male and safety.

"Did you find him?" I asked in a rush when we broke the kiss.

"I found him. He was all right when I left."

I sighed.

"The Nalian ship is taking him away now, with a few friends."

My mouth fell open. "Wait! How?"

The smug smile wouldn't leave his face. "I made a deal." When I kept waiting for an answer, he just said, "I can be very persuasive."

I kissed him hard again.

Then we'll die fighting. In very different ways, neither my brother nor I needed to live that way anymore.

"I love you," I said.

He gave me a look that sent slick heat to my core. "Not more than I love you, Vilet," he said, so low it sounded like a growl.

"Our cabin's over there." I let go of his neck with one arm to point.

With a swift motion, he swept my legs out from under me.

I squealed as he carried me the rest of the way.

"A lake," he said. "Have you seen any ducks yet?"

"Only a couple."

He took a few more long strides toward the beach. "This one?" It was the only little house in this area, so I wasn't sure why he asked.

I giggled. "Yes."

He opened the rounded green door. Once we got inside, he set me down and pushed me against the wall. One hand closed the door and the other formed a fist near my head as he kissed me.

"What do you want?" he asked between kisses.

"I want you naked in our bed."

"Where is that?" He picked me up again. I directed him to the right room. This place was one of the smaller houses, but it still felt enormous compared to anything I'd lived in before.

"Two slaps," he said before plopping me down on the soft covers.

I almost said, "I don't need them", which was true, but I liked hanging onto them as a reminder.

Together we scrambled for hems and buckles. We needed nothing between us. Just skin. Just breath. Just him moving inside me.

"Sit with your back against the headboard, on your knees," I ordered. My center was so wet by now it demanded his thick cock.

He listened, and I straddled him. His erection bounced against my stomach, so picked it up and guided it into me. Leander's small gasp made me drip with arousal. I exhaled as he seated himself fully inside me. Together, in small movements, we began grinding together, finding a rhythm. This way, I could watch his face the whole time. He wasn't the only one thrusting or sucking this time. We found our way together, not losing a single moment to see that dimple appear, or his forehead start to sheen with sweat, or the flex of his muscles as he maneuvered me on his lap. His smallest noise or movement fascinated me, made me want more.

He hit a sensitive spot greedy for friction. I shuddered and sucked in a breath.

"There?" he panted, doubling down.

I couldn't answer. I was whimpering, head thrown back, as the world became that one point that needed more, more, *oh gods I can't take it*, more!

A tremor shook my body with release.

Leander must have been waiting, because he puffed out a held breath and thrust upward more frantically, slowing only in loud groans of relief. He tilted his head back against the wall.

I kissed his throat tenderly and rolled off him with all the grace of a flopping fish now on land. We sat side by side, breathing heavily. On the opposite wall were two shelves of bread and vegetables. I knew they belonged in the kitchen, but seeing them every morning when I woke up reminded me that I didn't have to be hungry or scared or alone.

I took Leander's hand. "You know what I thought yesterday?"

"Hm?" His eyes were heavy-lidded, glazed with pleasure.

"You're a demi-god and I'm a human. Even if I lived a long life, I would have gotten old and died, and you would stay like this." I placed my palm on his scarred chest muscles.

He picked up my hand and kissed the palm.

"It's not... good, what happened," I continued. "But now I'm this way forever, and we can be on more equal footing."

"Equal footing?" He shook off some of the sleepiness. "That was never the problem. I knew you were human from the second I met you. You were just such a resilient, funny, brave, sexy human that I couldn't help myself."

I laughed. "But you have to admit, this wouldn't have worked if—"

"Maybe," he conceded.

"If we weren't here, together, this way."

He considered it a moment. "I like you that way." A kiss. "And this way." A kiss. "And any way you become in the future. It's your heart, Vilet. Eriset didn't ruin it."

Watching this gorgeous warrior call me brave brought a lump to my throat. I'd only tried to outlast the danger around me, like everybody else I knew.

"It ruined me," he murmured, "but you showed me hope." This time, his kiss was warm and wet and long.

"Thank you for bringing me here," I whispered, bringing my hand to his cheek. "You are my safe, Leander."

His eyes went wicked. "Let me show you how much I adore you for that statement."

"Like with a snack?"

His gaze drifted down my body. "A snack. A whole meal."

"I mean a real one."

He blinked. "What?"

"Bread and butter, grapes, cheese. We have wine."

"You're hungry right now?" Leander looked genuinely confused.

I laughed and gave him a kiss. "Yes, I'm usually hungry.

And I want to do everything with you, even normal things. Don't worry, it's just a break from..." I glanced at his dick, which was already hard again.

"Every position," he recited, as if he'd thought about it. "Every fantasy you've ever had." He made his way toward the food shelves.

"Yes," I said through a smile.

All of it. I would have all of it with this strong, ridiculous, protective, experienced demi-god.

But first, the simple pleasure of snuggling in bed with a full belly and the knowledge that Ares and his armies could never threaten us again. Our future, and the future of those I loved, was secure.

Leander poured us two glasses of wine and returned to the bed. I nestled between his legs so I could lean against him and he could hold me around the middle. We clinked our glasses. This was more than contentment. Contentment was soft and warm like a breeze. This moment pitched higher, jolting through me with the strength of grief, except this time it was the opposite. A laugh escaped my stained lips.

"What is it?" Leander asked.

I twisted to look up at him and caress his cheek. "I'm just really happy."

He smiled down at me before pressing a soft kiss to my forehead. "I'm really happy too."

This first book in the Deathless Love series welcomes you to the Eight Realms, where danger and desire lurk in every corner, and mythology isn't quite as you remember it.

Join the Foxy newsletter and read this book FREE!

Juniper loves her boyfriend Luca. There's just one problem (in the eyes of Far Realm society, anyway.) She's a faun and he's a vampire.

When Juniper asks him if she can attend the full moon ritual, he's horrified. The ritual is for vampire clans to unleash their most primal urges—no place for a faun. But either she goes with him, putting herself in danger and letting her see the worst sides of him, or their relationship stalls.

Luca is afraid he'll lose her either way, but Juniper hopes he'll finally let her see this last private piece of his heart.

Will their love for each other be enough to withstand one night with the vampire clan?

"Do you believe in perfect mates?"

"No."

I crunched another walnut. "You don't? I read today that all vampires believe in one true soulmate."

Luca eyed me with amused suspicion. He folded his black wings, adjusting his reading position in the velvet chair. "And I heard that all fauns live in the forest. We're not all the same, Juniper."

"I wasn't saying you're all the same."

"And you've known that fact for ages. Before you read it today for the Assembly."

I pursed my lips. He caught me. "Well, yes."

"So why are you bringing it up now?" He set down the book he was reading—*Salts and Spice*—and beckoned me onto his lap.

I couldn't resist. Not with that smooth voice and those deep-set eyes. The slightest movement in them conveyed profound depth and emotion. A crinkle in the corners meant laughter. The barest downturn of his dark eyebrows meant deep hurt. An unflinching, sparkling stare meant he wanted my clothes off.

Settling onto his strong thighs, I saw a hint of that look. "You've never mentioned it."

"That vampires believe in perfect mates? Is that something you would talk about all the time?"

He was talking around an answer. Luca had his mysteries, but I didn't think this would be one of them.

I had to be careful talking about his vampire heritage. He kept parts of his vampirism secret from me, which drove me mad. Plus, not everyone thought I was smart to fall for a vampire. Flings happened, but not love. Not with a faun. I didn't want to be seen as prey by people who saw us together. Despite being a vampire through a through, Luca didn't see me that way, and that was the important thing.

He caressed the place below my knee where my skin gave way to soft brown fur.

"I would talk about it with you," I insisted. "I wouldn't leave you to do your own research when an expert lived right here."

The comment hit its mark too well. His eyes darkened with annoyance. "You like doing research," he said silkily. Half ice, half warmth. "You know plenty about vampires, and even more about me."

Lamplight traced his high pale cheekbones and shadowed his black hair. He lightly shook out one wing.

"Are you uncomfortable?" I asked. The high back of the chair wasn't the best choice for the house, in retrospect, because Luca's wings might get cramped behind him. "We can move."

Luca laughed, the ice from a moment ago shattering. "Holding you? No, I'm not uncomfortable." Moonlight streamed through the window, adding ghostly blue to the lamplight. He fished in his pocket and pulled out a salt bead. The quick flash of his fangs caught the light as he threw it in his mouth and sucked. "Most ways."

He needed more salt beads with the full moon coming. They replaced his craving for blood. By now, I associated the taste of salt with Luca's lips.

"You're always wondering if I'm uncomfortable, if I need

something," he said, leaning in. "You should think more about yourself."

"I always think about myself and how I can earn us more money."

"We don't need more money." His voice was a seductive murmur. "I don't need anything but you. And I can think of a way I'd be more comfortable."

My heart skittered. Wasn't the full moon still a week away? Usually, he didn't get this demanding until a couple days before. I loved when he took control and lost control at once, but most of the time he didn't allow himself to. It was for the best, he assured me, but I knew his self-control had something to do with his vampire past. He was protecting me, but I'd prefer the truth to safety.

My thoughts melted away as his hot breath feathered over my mouth. His salty, cool scent filled my lungs the instant before his lips met mine. And it wasn't just his lips. His strong hands positioned me so I straddled him. One hand pressed my upper back and the other dominated my hip, pulling me up until I could feel his hard bulge against my pulsing core. Then he rocked us, grinding us together, rubbing my sensitive, wet clit.

His exhales became growls and grunts. Mine became whimpers. His bat-like wings contracted around us with arousal.

I rolled my hips faster in a circular motion we both went crazy for. Finally, he tore off the kiss and my underwear, freed his cock and impaled me on it.

"Ah!" I cried, letting my head fall back as he thrust up in deeper and wilder strokes.

He licked a long line up my throat, then another, lapping up the sweat as we worked together, straining to get closer, to get friction on the sopping, swollen places.

I lost myself in him. There was his length inside me and his tongue on my neck and his strong, searching hands in my hair, on my ass, scratching my thighs, gripping my breasts...

My cries grew higher, higher. With a firm shove upward, he broke me. I exploded into blackened, piercing stars.

Luca was still feral, finishing, when I came to. Pulling out at the last moment, he shot cum on my lower belly.

Without him inside me, I could felt just how damn wet I was. My juices were getting all over Luca's tailored pants. But on full moon weeks, he never cared. On full moon weeks, like this one, he'd draw his finger across my pussy one more time and suck off the wet. Like he did now.

"Mmmm," he moaned. "You're the most delicious thing I've ever tasted, Juniper."

I flushed even hotter when he got all hoarse and wild like that. My name in his mouth sounded like sin.

"You cook every day," I teased.

Luca smirked, those expressive eyes dancing. "No spices taste like you, Jun."

Too bad he didn't believe in perfect mates, because I could have sworn he was mine.

ORDER FULL MOONS AND VAMPIRES TODAY!

READ MORE BY ZORA FOX

Fae and Shadow duology
    End of the Forest
    Trapped by the Fae

Deathless Love series
    Wings and Blindness
    Flowers and the Far Realm
    Storm and Sanctuary
    Flame and Warpaint
    Full Moons and Vampires (coming soon!)

Find all of Zora Fox's spicy fantasy romance titles on Amazon.